AF306748

Defoe
Abbott
Marx
Hardy
Melville
Montaigne
Machiavelli
Haggard
Chesterton
Cooper
Emerson
Joyce
Austen
Hugo
Eliot
Grimm
Stoker
Carroll
Christie
Maupassant
Byron
Engels
Molière
Schiller
Wilde
Garnett
Einstein
Fitzgerald
Hawthorne
Smith
Kafka
Goethe
Dostoyevsky
Hall
Cotton
Kipling
Doyle
Willis
Baum
Henry
Nietzsche
Balzac
Leslie
Dumas
Flaubert
Turgenev
Stockton
Vatsyayana
Crane
Burroughs
Verne
Curtis
Tocqueville
Gogol
Vinci
Homer
Widger
Tolstoy
Whitman
Busch
Darwin
Thoreau
Twain
Potter
Freud
Zola
Lawrence
Scott
Plato
Harte
Kant
Jowett
Stevenson
Dickens
Hesse
Andersen
Burton
London
Descartes
Cervantes
Voltaire
Poe
Aristotle
Wells
Cooke
Hale
James
Hastings
Bunner
Shakespeare
Irving
Richter
Chambers
da
Shaw
Doré
Dante
Chekhov
Wodehouse
Benedict
Alcott
Swift
Pushkin
Newton

Cad Metti, The Female Detective Strategist Dudie Dunne Again in the Field

Harlan Page Halsey

Imprint

This book is part of TREDITION CLASSICS

Author: Harlan Page Halsey
Cover design: Buchgut, Berlin – Germany

Publisher: tredition GmbH, Hamburg - Germany
ISBN: 978-3-8472-3033-5

www.tredition.com
www.tredition.de

CHAPTER I.

TWO SKILLFUL YOUNG DETECTIVES OVERMATCH A BRACE OF VILLAINS AND PROVE WHAT NERVE AND COURAGE CAN DO.

"Let's duck him and steal the girl."

A young lady and gentleman were walking on the sands at Coney Island beach. The lady was very handsomely at [Pg 5] tired, and by her side walked a young man, a perfect type in appearance of an effeminate dude. Three rough-looking men had been following the lady and gentleman at a distance, and when the latter stopped at a remote part of the beach far from any hotel the three men held a consultation, and one of them uttered the declaration with which we open our narrative.

As usual certain very exciting incidents led up to the scene we have depicted. One week prior to the meeting on the beach a young detective known as Dudie Dunne, owing to the fact that he often assumed the rôle of a dude as a throw-off, was seated in a hotel smoking-room when a shrewd-faced, athletic-looking man approached him and said:

"Hello, Dunne! I've been on the lookout for you."

"You've found me."

"I have, and I'm glad. I've got a great shadow for you."

"I am all ears, Wise."

"I want you in the government service. There is a chance for you to make a big hit."

"I am ready to make a big hit, Wise."

"You are in a position to do it. You speak Italian, but what is better, you have your lady pal. She is a real Italian, I am told, and one of the bravest and brightest women that ever entered the profession."

"Some one told you that?"

"Yes."

"Whoever did so knew what they were talking about. Cad Metti is one of the brightest women that ever entered the profession; she is a born detective. What is the job?"

"There is a gang at work—the worst ever known. They are Italians, but they have a contingent of American and English rogues working with them. They are [Pg 6] the most dangerous operators that ever organized for the coining of base money. They are located all over the United States. They have regular passwords. Indeed, their organization is perfect, and with them are a number of desperate assassins, and a few beautiful women. I can't go into all the details, but the government has appropriated a large sum from the secret service fund. We must run down and break up this dangerous gang."

"You have the case in hand?"

"I am directing the hunt. I have twenty of my best men on the case, and I have trailed down to the fact that all the movements are directed from New York. The chief men are located here, and never in the history of criminal doings was such a dangerous lot at work."

"What points have you?"

"The only point I have is the fact that the leaders are located here in New York."

"In what line are they working?"

"They are counterfeiting in all its branches, they are bank robbing and burglarizing private houses. Indeed every sort of criminal appears to be in the organization. It is not even confined to the United States. They are sending base American money to Mexico and Cuba. The president of the Mexican republic has sent a large sum here to aid in their capture. The merchants of Havana have also sent on a fund."

"And you have no clues as to the identity of these people?"

"We have captured several of the gang, but that does not interrupt the work. It's the leaders we want, and if you can get in and trail them down it will be the biggest feather you ever wore in your cap. But let me tell you, it's a dangerous job. Several of our men have mysteriously vanished. Two we know were assassinated; the others have been done away with. My reputation is at stake. Thus far I have been baffled." [Pg 7]

"And what do you want me to do?"

"Shadow down and locate the leaders."

"Can you give me a hint where to look for them? That is, can you give me any starter at all?"

"I cannot. You may find them mingling in the best society in New York; you may find them in the slums under cover. One thing is certain: they are the shrewdest rascals that ever defied the whole detective force of the United States, and I have great hopes that you can succeed where we have all failed. You can command me for all the money you need; and now get in and run down these rogues."

"You have no photographs?"

"No."

"You say there are women in with the gang?"

"Yes."

"Here in New York?"

"Yes."

"Are the women shoving the queer?"

"If they do they do it so well we cannot trace them; but there are women in the gang."

"Have they a workshop here?"

"I do not think they have. I believe the workshop is in some remote place, possibly in Mexican territory; but the leaders are here, and it is necessary to trail down the leaders and get the evidence against them. If we get the leaders we can knock out the whole gang. My men have located members of the gang, and we can close in on them any time, but none of them will squeal as long as the leaders go free. But once let us secure the leaders and there will follow a wholesale squeal, and we can break up the gang."

"All right, I am in with you. I will see Cad Metti and talk the matter over with you later on."

"I should like to meet your female pal." [Pg 8]

During the time Wise, the great special, had been talking to Dunne a district messenger lad had been standing near munching on a cracker which he had taken from the free lunch table, and at the proper moment he stepped forward and handed our hero a note.

The latter glanced at the missive and said:

"All right, lad; there is no answer."

The boy stood around and finally Dunne handed him a nickel. The boy laughed, said "thank you," and walked away, and Dunne said:

"You have never seen Cad Metti?"

"No."

"Are you sure?"

"Why, certainly, I'd know if I had ever seen her."

"You would?"

"Yes."

"Wise, your memory fails you."

"I've never been accused of loss of memory."

"You never have?"

"No."

"And yet you've seen Cad Metti."

"Never."

"You are sure."

"Certainly."

"You saw her once talking to me."

"Never."

"Come, come, I'll bet you a cigar."

"No use to bet; I tell you I've never seen the girl."

"Then bet."

"All right, I'll bet."

"And you've never seen her?"

"Never."

"But you did see her once, and as an old detective with his eyes always peeping I supposed you recognized her."

"I reckon I would have recognized her if I had ever [Pg 9] seen her. You have some other officer in your mind whom you confound with me."

"No, you once saw her with me. She was under cover, but of course you would fall to that."

"But I've never seen her."

"Then it's a bet?"

"Yes."

"You saw Cad Metti within the last five minutes."

"I did?"

"Yes."

"Where?"

"That you should know. I tell you that you have seen her."

"I say I never have."

"You think you would have recognized her?"

"Yes."

"Under any cover?"

"Yes."

"You have seen her all the same."

Wise was thoughtful a moment and then exclaimed:

"Great Scott! it is impossible."

"No, sir."

"Do you mean to tell me that— —"

"Yes, I mean to tell you that the messenger lad was Cad Metti."

"Great Cæsar! Oscar Dunne, that girl is a marvel."

"Well, she is."

"I've heard how you first met her."

"Yes, and I've been her instructor. She is, I will admit, the most wonderful girl I ever met. Did I say met? I will add I never read or heard of such a girl. She could make her living on the stage as a marvel. She is a great musical genius. She can sing or dance, she can fence or wrestle like a man. Her strength is extraordinary, and as a pistol shot she is the champion woman of the world; [Pg 10] and when it comes to quickness, nerve, cunning, and courage she cannot be excelled."

"I reckon you are dead in love with your pal."

"You needn't do any guessing on that score. She is my detective aid and together we will perform wonders for you. I will talk the matter over with Cad. We will lay out a plan and I will report to you."

"Good enough; I feel hopeful. It will be a great thing to run down this gang, for, as I said, they are the most dangerous lot of criminals on earth, and their head-center is evidently a man of genius. Let us catch him and we will easily close down on the whole gang."

"Cad and I will locate him, you bet."

"And get the evidence?"

"I reckon when we get him we will get the evidence along with him. You know it will be a hunt for evidence that will lead up to the capture."

"Oscar, you are not slow at the business."

"Thank you; but it's business and not compliments."

"Good enough; I expect to hear from you."

"I'll report."

"Will you have your cigar?"

"Yes, I won; I'll take it."

Oscar Dunne was a young detective who had earned a great reputation. Some of our readers have read an account of his previous exploits and know what a smart chap he is. Those who have not read about Dudie Dunne we advise to do so. As stated in our previous account, Oscar had no particular history. He had simply graduated to the detective force, and had made a great success; and as also stated, he was a young man of singularly effeminate appearance, with muscles like a whipcord and powers of endurance that were seemingly tireless. He was not only a great athlete but a wonderful boxer, and it was a favorite role with him to assume the character of a dude, and [Pg 11] many a surprise he had given to various smart Alecs during his career on the force, and with the surprise he generally administered when required a good sound drubbing to some fellow who had set him down as an exquisite. His looks when in the "dude cover" were very deceiving, and when he started in to throw off his mask he became a terror to evil-doers, and at the time when we introduce him a second time to our readers he had won a great reputation as a singularly successful detective officer.

Shortly after parting with Wise, the great government special, Oscar went on to the street, and proceeding up town entered a very respectable-looking house which he entered with a night key. It was his home. He had made considerable money and had provided a home for himself. The house outside was very unpretentious, but inside it was as luxurious as the home of a rich bachelor. We will here state for the information of our readers who are making their first acquaintance with Oscar Dunne that in a great case in which he had been engaged he met a beautiful Italian girl who aided him very materially. The girl earned a good reward and when Oscar asked her what she proposed to do her answer was:

"I shall become a detective," and then and there a partnership was formed between Oscar Dunne and Caroline Metti. The latter lived with a countrywoman who had kept boarders, but who was only too glad to give up her general boarding business to become a housekeeper for Cad Metti, the latter having rescued and adopted two Italian children from the street, a boy and girl, whom she had determined to educate and advance in life in case both proved worthy.

Cad Metti's home was not far from the residence of her male professional partner, and the pair were in constant communication. Oscar was an adept at disguises, and he had found in Cad Metti a ready scholar, and be [Pg 12] tween them they had studied the art of disguise as a science and both had become very versatile and proficient.

As stated, Oscar went direct to his rooms after parting from Wise, the government special, and a few moments later a veiled lady appeared at his door and was shown into his sitting-room. Oscar's housekeeper was a sister of his mother, a motherly old lady, to whom the detective had given a home. The veiled lady entered the house in a manner that might have suggested to a countryman that she was one of the family. She entered the sitting-room, as indicated, and throwing aside her veil stood revealed in all her magnificent youthful beauty.

"Cad," said our hero, "I am glad you have come."

The female detective, who had removed her veil, smiled a dazzling smile and said:

"I thought you might wish to see me."

"I always wish to see you, but this time it is on business."

"Then let's follow the advice you have often given: spare compliments and talk business."

Oscar proceeded and related to his lady pal word for word all that had passed between the government special and himself. The female detective listened with deep attention, and when the narrative was concluded said:

"I think we can locate this man."

"I think we can; but how shall we start in?"

Cad was thoughtful a moment and then said:

"In our old way."

"How is that?"

"Chum for them."

This criminal "chumming" has yielded good returns, as a rule. It is the best card in the detective profession.

"Where shall we chum?"

"Everywhere."

"I'll put it straight. Where shall we start in?" [Pg 13]

Again the beautiful Cad Metti pondered, and after an interval said:

"Criminals as a rule are fond of race betting."

"That's so."

"We've picked up many a clue down at the race track."

"We have."

"Let's try a little chumming down there. Good races are on, and if ever our bluefish show up at the track they will do so this present week."

"And we'll lure them as they swim, eh?"

"That's it."

"How will we make up?"

"You are to became Dudie Dunne. I will become Silly Sal."

"And we'll bet on the races?"

"We will."

"It's a go, Cad. To-morrow we will take in the races and chum for our game."

On the following day the two detectives, well gotten up for their "chumming" scheme, started down for the Sheepshead Bay track.

They went on the course and played the rôle they had determined to play to perfection. They attracted considerable attention and that was what they most desired, for it was their "chumming" game to bring around the fish.

CHAPTER II.

CAD METTI AND OSCAR DUNNE DO SOME FINE "CHUMMING" AND SUCCEED IN BRING- ING A BIG FISH TO NIBBLE AT THEIR BAIT.

Oscar Dunne and Cad Metti were indeed great experts in enacting a rôle. They took a seat in the grand [Pg 14] stand and through a messenger boy bet on the races. They won, and they laughed and tittered in delight over their success, and, as intimated, attracted a great deal of attention, and they exhibited considerable money. Oscar was playing the rôle of a dude with plenty of "stuff," as the vulgar phrase puts it, and Cad was playing the rôle of a fast young girl who was leading the exquisite fool to squander his roll. Well, it was a great chumming game well played—played before a lot of men who were as avaricious as impecunious gamblers always are. There were men there who bet and lost. There were men there who had no money to risk, and they all thought themselves possessed of brains, and here was a silly fool loaded with money, and here also was a silly girl reaping a rich harvest in greenbacks from her enamored dude, *as it appeared*, and so the game went on until a man with a keen eye got them under his glance. He stood awhile and watched them, and various expressions passed over his face. After a little the man strolled away. He joined two other men, and going close to them he said in a low tone:

"I've struck a chance to make a raise."

"Good enough," was the response.

"Yes, and it's dead easy."

"What is it?"

"I'll go over opposite the grand stand; you fellows follow me. Come up offhand and I'll show where a big haul lies right in sight."

The rogues had struck a lead and so had the two sharp-eyed detectives who were playing such a neat game.

"Cad," said Oscar, "we've got a bite."

"Yes, I felt the nibble."

"It's a good thing, sis, to locate a rogue."

"Indeed it is."

"We have not chummed in vain." [Pg 15]

"So it would appear."

This little bit of side talk was carried on while the two detectives maintained the role they were enacting, and a little while later they saw the three join each other and beheld them as furtively they watched their anticipated prey.

"We've got three bites, Cad."

"I see them."

"What shall we do?"

"Don't ask me to suggest, Oscar. No one can beat you in laying out plans."

"We'll leave here."

"And learn if they follow?"

"Yes."

"That would be my idea."

"Where shall we go?"

"We will give them a chance to follow us. We will go to the beach."

Oscar and Cad did not start right off—they were too smart for that. They were playing a great game. They did not see the three men; they did not know they were being watched. Oh, no, they were too absorbed in each other and the fun they were having and the winnings they were raking in. It was a strange incident, but one that often occurs. Oscar was not betting to win. He was merely betting as a "guy," and, as intimated, it often happens that the careless win where the careful and posted lose. A race had just been run and a messenger boy returned with the tickets he had cashed, and the girl pulled out a big wad of bills and added the winnings to her roll. The three observers noticed that she carried the bulk of the money, and one of them said:

"Great sea waves! what a wad she has got!"

"And here we are, chummies, dead broke—not been able to make a bet." [Pg 16]

"Not a bet," came the doleful refrain.

"We'll bet to-morrow," said one of the men with a knowing wink.

"That depends."

"On what?"

"They may have a coach down here and outride us."

"Don't you believe it. That chap is too happy. He'll have the gal down to the beach for a supper. Good enough, we will take our supper later on. He'll treat; yes, we'll dine with him without an invitation—see?"

"I don't see it yet."

"Well, just watch. Aha! what did I say? They've had enough of the race; they are going. Good enough; I'll bet my share of the swag they go for a ramble."

"How will we manage it?"

"We'll just lay low and learn what our chances are. They are getting very reckless, they are. Eh! the girl may want his watch and sparkles. If she does she will lead him away off for a long walk. She'll nip the sparkles and the watch, and then, my covies, what will we do?"

"We'll nip her, eh?"

"You bet. Now just watch. There they go. Who was right, eh?"

"I reckon you were, old man."

"You bet I am, every time. Ah, we're in luck."

Oscar occasionally got a sly chance to glance at the three thieves, and so cute was he, and such a face reader, he could almost have repeated their talk without hearing a word of it. He read their conversation on their well-marked faces.

"Let's go, Cad. We've got them well hooked. They have seen your wad; that's what they are measuring."

The girl tittered. It was her way of working off her excitement in view of the adventure she knew they were to pass through; and indeed a very startling adventure was to crown the incidents of the day and night. [Pg 17]

Oscar and Cad left their seats and had wandered like a pair of happy young lovers toward the exit gate, and they were the observed of all observers. Many remarks, pertinent and characteristic, were made concerning them, and yet, seemingly unconscious that they were attracting any attention at all, they moved along. Upon reaching the platform they met a train that had just arrived from the city, and boarded it to make the short run to the Island. And all the time they maintained their frivolous demeanor, but four sharp eyes were on the alert, and Oscar observed:

"They are swallowing the bait."

"Yes, we've got 'em."

It's strange, but about the same idea ran through the minds of the three rogues. They had feared that their game might take a train to the city, and when they saw them board the train bound for the Island the man who had spotted the game said:

"What did I tell you, covies?"

"They are going to the beach."

"They are, dead sure."

"We are in luck."

"We are, you bet, and now I am going to prophesy again. That gal has got a good thing. I tell you she will walk him away off down the beach. She is bound to have those sparkles. She has her eye on them. Good enough; I hope she'll get 'em, but she'll never wear 'em. No, no, it's I and you, my covies, who will wear those sparkles. We covets them, we do, and we's got to have 'em; yes, sir, we's got to have 'em, and we will."

Oscar saw the man get on a rear car, as intimated, and there was triumph in his heart.

We will here explain the theory upon which the confederate detectives were working. Wise had said that there was an organized gang, that the scoundrels were practic [Pg 18] ing all manner of criminality, and he had determined upon the link by link game—a good one—a search for clues. One thief as a rule knows another thief, and so the linking of acquaintance goes on until a rogue is struck who suggests a participation. The rule does not always work, but generally it is a success, and was likely to prove so in the "shadow" Oscar was working. He knew he might get on to the trail of a dozen or more rogues before he struck one that was a member of the secret criminal organization. He had every reason to hope he would succeed.

The confederate detectives arrived at the Manhattan Beach Hotel, and as our hero had resolved to move very slowly and take notes as he went along he led Cad to a table and ordered a dinner, and during the meal the same amusing farce was kept up, and the thieves passed and repassed the table where their selected victims were seated.

"They are following down to a close shadow on us," said Oscar.

"Yes, and I am looking forward to the surprise we have in store for them."

"It will be very enjoyable; but, Cad, I've been thinking."

"I call you down before you speak."

"What was I going to say?"

"You were going to say there was risk, and I must not scare it."

"Partner, you are a mind reader."

"I can read your mind when it runs in a generous direction."

"It is not a matter of generosity but of precaution. Those fellows look like a desperate trio."

"Certainly, but they are off their guard."

"They are?" [Pg 19]

"Yes."

"How?"

"Oh, you know well enough, we've acted so as to throw them off. Do you know how they have measured us?"

"I have an idea. What is yours?"

"They think you are a flat."

"That's certain."

"They think I am playing you."

"Right again."

"They think a slight rap on the ear will send you squealing."

"Yes, that's correct."

"Then they will go through me, and as I am, as they believe, a thief like themselves they fear no risk from me."

"Admitting what you say is true — —"

"We will give them a great surprise."

"Sure, but after they discover their mistake — —"

"It will be too late for them to do any harm. We will have them flattened out, or we will have forgotten an old way of managing these things. Oscar, it is a great thing to meet an antagonist who really underrates you."

"That is true."

"And so in this deal I tell you I think we are on a better lay than we are aware of. After we have downed these fellows we will know what to do."

"Yes, we will follow them up."

"Certainly, and we will have a great lead."

Oscar and Cad lingered a long time at the table. They desired "wind and tide," as we will put it, to be just right for them.

It was well on toward five o'clock when the confederate detectives rose from the dinner table and walked down toward the beach. They walked very slowly and all the time maintained the rôle they had started out to assume. [Pg 20] They passed the bathing pavilion, walked along beyond the Oriental Hotel and then turned toward the beach at a point bordering on the inlet, and there they halted and stood to admire the incoming waves. Twilight was beginning to cast its lengthening shadows over land and sea.

The men who were set to rob the couple meantime dodged along on their trail, keeping far in shore toward the Sheepshead Bay, and their leader was chuckling all the time. He said:

"Oh, covies! how am I for a prophet? I'm a mind reader, and I'll set up for a professional. These fagots are carrying out my programme to the letter. I tell you I know the ways of smart gals like the one who has that poor dude in tow. She is going for him right smart. She will clean him out. I shouldn't be surprised if she sandbagged him and left him lying on the beach. Well, well, won't we have a haul! I saw that wad, and I tell you it's a big one; and the watch and the diamonds! Ay, ay, we will just have a jolly time for a week. Talk about betting, eh! well, this little trick beats all betting. We play to win, not to lose, every time. There is no chance here. That gal is walking the dude right into our trap. We've got the wad already, and won't we have a surprise for the smart, bright-eyed little miss! Why, she is laying out her cash already, she is so sure of getting all the chap has; but we'll do the shopping on his wad, not she, you bet."

As stated, Oscar and Cad wandered down to the beach and here as before they enacted their rôle to perfection, and it was at this moment that one of the men asked:

"How shall we do it?"

It was then the man uttered the words with which we open our narrative:

"Let's duck him and steal the girl."

The three laughed. It all looked so easy. The young [Pg 21] fellow was, as they supposed, such a "sweetie," such a little darling, who would turn pale and plead for mercy the instant one of the three men spoke to him. The latter discussed their plan, and it was arranged that their leader should approach the young people and engage them in conversation. The man did approach and Oscar remarked to Cad:

"Now the fun commences. Well, well, what a real pretty surprise we have in store for those rogues! Cad, I enjoy this; yes, I do—it's immense!"

"Don't forget yourself, Oscar, and laugh too soon."

"Don't fear me, but there will be two or three sore heads around here in a few moments."

Meantime the man approached. The two detectives did not appear to see him until he stood directly in front of them and said:

"Good-day."

Oscar elevated his glasses to his eyes and stared at the man in true dude style, and Cad recoiled as though shocked at being addressed by a stranger.

"I beg your pardon, my friend," said Oscar, "I haven't the pleasure of your acquaintance."

"Oh, you haven't?"

"No, I can't say that I ever saw you before."

"Is that so?"

"Indeed it is true, my friend."

"What a pity! why, we are old friends."

The thief's pals were drawing near.

"You are mistaken, my friend," said Oscar, adding: "And I must kindly request you to move off and not disturb us."

The man haw-hawed in a rough manner and said:

"Well, you are playing it nice."

"I do not understand your allusion, sir. It is very vulgar—yes, sir, very vulgar." [Pg 22]

"Is it, indeed? Why, you rat, do you think I do not recognize you?"

"You certainly do not recognize me. I never saw you before in my life."

"He! he! ha! ha! that's great, my covie; yes, that's great. So you never saw me before? Well, well, I've seen you often enough. I was looking at your portrait only yesterday."

"You were looking at my portrait only yesterday?" repeated Oscar.

"Yes."

"Where on earth did you see my portrait?"

"In the rogues' gallery—number one hundred and three. Yes, yes, you rascal, I've run you down nicely; but see here, you and that girl appear to be enjoying yourselves and I don't wish to spoil your enjoyment. I am a gentleman, I am, and you can buy me off."

At this moment the rogue's pals approached, and the fellow turning toward them said:

"See here, this 'ere rat is pretending he don't know us. Eh! ain't that cool of him? And we have been a-follerin' of him this last two months and now we've caught him a-spendin' of the swag, and he's a-puttin' on airs. I say, miss, mebbe you don't know the character of the chappie who's a-spendin' his money on you so free. Mebbe you don't know he's a thief, and it's a part of his swag that you are having a fine time on; but I don't begrudge—no, I don't—the money that's gone, but youse must hand over the balance, or I'll be compelled to do my duty and take youse both in. Yes. I'll have to do my duty."

"My friend, you are evidently laboring under a great mistake."

"Am I now?"

"You certainly are." [Pg 23]

"Well, well, is that so?"

"It is the truth."

"See here, Johnny, I know you as the most expert pickpocket in the country. I've been on your track a long time. Now you can just pony up and go on with your flirtin'; otherwise you and the girl will go with me."

"Go with you?"

"That's it."

"Never! never! we would never permit ourselves to be seen in such company, you rough-looking boor, you."

"Hear him, boys, hear him! 'You rough-looking boor!' Well, he is a-puttin' on lugs, ain't he? What shall we do with him?"

"Duck him," came the answer.

CHAPTER III

A LIVELY SCENE FOLLOWS ON THE BEACH
AND THE THREE ROGUES GET WHAT HAD
BEEN PROMISED — A GREAT SURPRISE.

"My dear," said our hero, turning to his companion, "just hear these awful men! Did you ever hear anything like it? Why, they are really impertinent. Come, dear, we will go away and not talk with them further. It's a disgrace to be seen in their society a minute. Some of our friends might see us talking to these men and think they were our friends. Just to think of it!"

The three men laughed, and the leader mimicked:

"Yes, just to think of it! but see here, mister pickpocket, you can't work your high airs on us. I see you won't shell out, so we will just take you."

"Yes, in the water," said one of the men. "We'll duck him first, just to soften down his cheek a bit." [Pg 24]

"You wouldn't do that, would you?" said the leader.

"Yes, sure; the idea of him puttin' on airs, eh! yes, let's duck him."

"All right, comrade, it's as you say."

"Why, hear the horrid men," said Oscar. "Maybe they think it is a great joke to try and scare us, but we don't scare; do we, my dear?"

Cad did look as though she was almost scared out of her wits, and we desire to call our readers' attention to the courage and nerve of both the detectives in daring for one moment to think of meeting those three great burly men.

"Say, young fellow, just hand over the swag you've stolen so we can return it to the owner and we'll let you off. I've a list of the articles: a watch, some diamonds and money. We don't want to be hard on you. Peel out the stuff and we'll let you off; won't we, comrades?"

"I don't know about that. I think we should do our duty," said one of the men.

"Well, yes, but seein' they're having such a good time I haven't the heart to put them in jail."

"Just as you say, captain, just as you say."

"Say, young fellow, will you hand over the swag?"

"He! he! he! really, gentleman, what jokers you are! I know you are very funny, but I don't understand your jokes; indeed, I don't."

"You don't, eh?"

"No, no; he! he! he!"

"Is it a joke to go to jail?"

"He! he! he! how funny! now I see you want to scare us; but see here, I don't scare. I can prove that to you, and if you do not go away I shall be compelled to thrash you."

"What!" ejaculated the three men, giving utterance to real laughter. It really did sound comical for that appar [Pg 25] ently slender dude to threaten to thrash three burly men.

"So you'll thrash us, eh?"

"He! he! he! yes, you will compel me to thrash you if you don't go away. Why, this lady is very much annoyed. I cannot see her annoyed; certainly not, so go away and I'll not harm you."

"Hear him—hear him!" cried one of the rogues, and he added: "We'll have to duck him for insultin' us."

"Yes, we'll have to duck him."

"Let's do it."

The men leaped forward when one of the most extraordinary scenes that ever occurred followed. As the men leaped forward both Oscar and Cad drew short billies—drew them so quickly that the men did not observe them until they *felt* them. A complete change had come over the appearance and actions of Oscar and Cad. The former with an ease and quickness that was wonderful to behold dealt the leader of the rogues a smart tap on the head that caused him to lie down in the sand as though stricken with a pain where his digestive organs reside. Cad meantime played a single-note tattoo on the head of number two, and Oscar, after dropping the

first man, paid his compliments to number three, who also concluded to lie down without any premeditation whatever. It was, as We
have intimated, a most singular, startling and extraordinary scene,
and before the men could rise each received to turn a second rap,
when Oscar inquired:

"What shall we do with them, sis?"

"Drown them," came the answer.

"No, no, it would be too bad to toss such mean carcasses into pure
water."

"But they'll become salted," said the girl.

"I reckon we've salted them pretty well; let's stroll."

Oscar and Cad walked away, resuming the same smart girl and
dude rôle they had played ere they fell to and downed the burly
ruffians. [Pg 26]

It was a sight for a comic paper, after Oscar and Cad had wandered away, to behold the three ruffians rise and look at each other.
For a moment none of them spoke. They just looked, until one of the
party, who evidently was a sort of humorist, said:

"Cap, I don't think we'll go shopping with their wad to-day."

The other man fell to the spirit of the occasion and said:

"Well, cap, it was *easy*, yes, very easy *for them*."

The leader looked, yes, looked very *blue*.

"Well, did you ever!" he murmured.

"No, I never," came the response.

"What was it we struck?"

"I feel as though something had *struck me*," was the answer.

"My covies, we got it good."

"Did you? Well, I got it *bad*. Oh, how my head aches!"

"Who are they?"

"I'll never tell you, but it was the gal gave me my rap and she came down on me with the force of a Goliah, and I went down—see? I'm down yet."

"I don't understand," said the leader as he mopped the blood trickling from the wound in his head with his handkerchief.

"I'll never explain it to you," said the humorist.

"Hang me, but I can't think."

"Neither can I. My thoughts are wool-gathering, and no wonder, eh? By jiminy! what a settler I got, and I settled."

"They were playing us."

"Yes, they were playing us, and they had lots of fun rattling on my poor conk."

"But who are they?" [Pg 27]

"Mr. and Mrs. Giant, I reckon, and it came so quick that for a moment I thought I was in a ship and a squall had blown the mast over on me. But see here, pards, we'd better get up and git, or mebbe some of our misdeeds may rise up in judgment against us. Instead of our putting the dude in jail he may jug us."

"Right you are; let's scatter."

"Where will we meet?"

"In the city, and we'd better lay low. There is more in this little experience than a crack on the head. We're lucky if we get away."

The three men rose to their feet, held a few moments' talk and then scattered. Each man determined to make his way to the city on his own hook, and they considered it was possibly by hook or by crook that they would get there.

Oscar and Cad had disappeared. Indeed, the rogues had hardly dared look at each other or speak until the "singulars" had gotten out of sight.

Once well away Oscar said:

"All right, Cad, I must leave you now to shift for yourself awhile. I am going to finish up this business. We know where to meet."

"Yes."

They were standing in a hollow between two sandbanks and it was dark.

"Change," said Oscar.

Immediately there followed a most wonderful transformation. Cad Metti dropped her fine feathers as though by magic, and in her stead appeared a plain-looking country girl, while the dude vanished, and in his stead appeared a regular sporting appearing young fellow. No one would have recognized in either the two who had sat on the piazza of the hotel eating their dinner and cooing like two turtle-doves. [Pg 28]

"Well done," said Oscar as he gazed at the wonderful girl, Cad Metti, and an instant later he said:

"Now I will leave you. I must get on the track of those scoundrels."

Cad and Oscar did not stop to exchange farewells. The latter moved away rapidly toward the point where he had had the encounter with the three ruffians whom he and his female comrade had served out so well. Oscar desired to follow the leader and he arrived behind a rift of sand in time to watch them, and he was able to discern the fellow he desired to shadow. His man made a round-about tour toward the depot and then started afoot down the track, not daring to take the train at the Manhattan station. Our hero, however, proceeded to the station, knowing his man would board the train at Sheepshead Bay, and his conclusion was verified, for all three men had arrived at the Sheepshead Bay station and boarded the train as individuals, not exchanging one word. Indeed, all had worked a sort of half-and-half transform.

Oscar maintained his seat; he did not go to the car boarded by the men. He remained one car behind, but he was on the alert lest at any moment the rascals might desert the train, and so he arrived at Long Island City. The men went to the Twenty-third street boat, the detective followed them, and still they kept apart.

"Those fellows are scared," he muttered. "The surprise they got has taken all the life out of them."

Once in New York the special chap whom he was following walked up Twenty-third street to First avenue, then he turned down and finally entered a low tenement house. Oscar was at his heels and noted the house he entered, and took up a position directly opposite. There were lights in some of the front rooms, but the windows of the top floor front reflected no brilliance until a few moments after our hero had taken his position, when [Pg 29] there shot forth from the small windows a sickly gleam of light.

"Top floor front," was our hero's comment. He had located the room where the man had entered.

Oscar stood a little time revolving his next move in his mind, and finally he determined upon the old trick played so often and still played daily by officers on a quiet "lay."

He entered the tenement house and ascended the creaking stairs, and not a muscle in his sturdy form quivered, although it was a dangerous undertaking to enter that sort of a house on such an errand. There was a possibility that there were a dozen villains scattered around in the several apartments, for as the old saying has it, "Thieves flock together."

Oscar, however, was well-armed, cool, strong and agile, and he arrived in front of the door of the room and heard voices. He peeped in, as the keyhole was large and there was no key in the door. He saw the man to whom he had given the sore head, and a woman. The latter was a remarkable-looking person. She was about forty, as it appeared; her complexion was sallow, her features pointed, her eyes large and sunken, and the latter were very expressive, proving that the eagle-nosed woman was bright, alert and cunning. She wore a discontented look upon her face as she eyed the man who had entered her presence, and while Oscar peeped and listened he heard her say:

"I am tired of this."

"Tired of what?"

"Do you want to know?"

"Yes, I do."

"I'll tell you. I am tired of living in these rooms; tired of going hungry; tired of wearing old clothes; tired of slaving for you—a miserable fake."

"Hold on, Sarah, don't talk to me that way." [Pg 30]

"Yes, I will talk to you that way. When I met you, I had plenty of money. You pretended to love me and I was fool enough to accept your love. I let you have money. I had a good, comfortable home, and now where am I? You have squandered every penny on the races. You don't know how to gamble, and yet you gamble away every cent you get. You do not come home when you have a stake and say, 'Here, my dear, is a hundred or two for you.' No, no, you come in and dole me out a few stamps and say, 'Make yourself comfortable.' In fact, when you have a good stake you do not come home at all, if this miserable place can be called a home. Tom, I'll stand it no longer; you and I will separate."

"Hold on, Sarah, do not talk that way."

"Yes, I will talk that way, and I will act. I can make plenty of money. No need for me to stay here and play wife to a man who only cares for himself and who hasn't the courage to start in and make a good haul and give me the comforts I've been accustomed to enjoy; and as you can't do it I'll start out and win them for myself, and I will not furnish you money to gamble while I starve here in these rooms without food, fire or clothing. I tell you I am through."

The man Tom was thoughtful a moment and then said:

"Sarah, all you say is true, but I've had no money."

"And you never will have."

"Yes, I will."

"Never."

"Why do you say so?"

"You haven't the courage; you are a coward."

"Hold, Sarah, I took a big chance this very afternoon to make a big stake. I showed all the courage, but got the worst of it. I ran up against a cyclone disguised as a gentle sea breeze, but I am going to have a big stake, and [Pg 31] all you need is just a little patience and

you shall have an elegant home, horses and carriages, and diamonds and servants."

"Oh, come off, Tom; no more fairy stories for me."

"It's no fairy story, Sarah. I tell you there is no one on earth that I
love as I do you. I've felt bad seeing you living this way and I've
done the best I could; but I am to be let into the greatest gang on
earth. I will make money from the start, and you will be let in and
we can in a few weeks make a big stake and skip. What I tell you is
no fairy story."

"Bah! Tom, I've heard your wild tales before."

"This is no wild tale. I tell you in a few weeks we will be flush."

The woman's eyes glittered as she said:

"I wish I could believe you, Tom."

"You can believe me."

"Why are you so secret about it? Why don't you open up?"

"I have not been initiated yet. It is the greatest gang that ever got
together."

"Do you know any of the parties in it?"

"Certainly I do. All countries are represented. We have the talent
of the world in it. The leaders are the smartest men on earth. They
have branches in every large city in the United States. They are in
with big politicians, judges and millionaires. They have defied the
police for eighteen months, and they are all ready to flood the land
and get away, and I am to be let in."

"Counterfeiters, Tom?"

"Well, yes, that is a part of their business. They counterfeit cur-
rency, metal and bonds, government and bank. They will make a
big general sweep. Every man in it will get his share, and a share is
a fortune. It's the most perfect organization ever effected, and I tell
you I [Pg 32] am to be in it among the big bugs too, and all through
you."

"All through me?"

"Yes."

"How is that?"

"They need you."

"They do?"

"Yes."

"In what capacity?"

"To sign the papers."

Again the woman's eyes glittered as she asked:

"How did they learn about me?"

"One of our old pals told them about you."

"And why did you not tell me about this before?"

"I have not had my first interview yet with the king-pin. He has been out West. He is to be in New York some day this week. You are to exhibit your skill and we will get a stake immediately."

"And you will gamble it away in an hour."

"No, I've sworn off."

"Bah! how many times you've told me that!"

"I mean it this time."

"Tom, I am fond of you, but I cannot let you ruin me again. If we make a big stake I am to hold the money. Do you hear?"

"Yes, I hear."

"And you understand that I mean what I say?"

"I do."

"I can beat the world on false signatures."

"That is what they have been told."

"I've long wanted a chance like this."

"I know it."

"I can make my own terms when they learn what I can do."

"I know it." [Pg 33]

Our readers can readily imagine the feelings of Dudie Dunne as he listened to this wonderful revelation. He realized that he and Cad Metti had made the hit of their lives, or rather had a chance to do so. It seemed wonderful that he had in this most astonishing manner gotten right on to the whole scheme, was peering, as it were, into the very heart of the terrible organization. It was not wholly skill that had brought him to this point; there was a large element of luck in it. Was it not more? Was there not fate in it, that through his ingenious strategy and Cad's suggestion he had followed the man of all men who under circumstances the most marvelous would bring him in contact with the king of the great criminal confederacy?

Oscar just reveled in his success. His face was actually radiant. The great special, Wise, had told him the best detectives in the land had been baffled. Wise himself had failed, and he had selected Oscar, and the young man was delighted at the prospect of maintaining the great special's confidence in his ability. Meantime the conversation continued.

"When are you to meet these people?"

"I don't know exactly. The king-pin is out West. He is liable to return any day."

"And then?"

"You are to give an exhibition of your skill."

The woman clasped her hands and casting her eyes to the floor exclaimed:

"Oh, how I have longed for a chance like this, Tom! I love luxury. I would be a handsome, yes, a splendid woman if I only had money. This is the best chance we ever had in our lives."

"Yes, Sarah, and I will be proud to see you dressed like a queen."

"Give me the money and I will dress like a queen; I [Pg 34] know how to dress. But who is with you in securing this great chance?"

"I will tell you all about it later on, Sarah. You can be hopeful, and now I will go to meet one or two of the boys. I will not be home again until early in the morning. We have a little job on hand. It may yield a few, bits for us; I can't tell."

"Tom, with the great chance we have, be careful. Do not get nipped just as our fortune is made."

CHAPTER IV.

OSCAR ENCOUNTERS A SERIES OF ADVENTURES IN FOLLOWING A PROMISING TRAIL AND MEETS WITH A PLEASANT SURPRISE.

Oscar slid down the stairs. His trick had been too good a one for him to take any chances. He did not wish to scare his bird off ere he had him bagged. He walked away and waited for Tom to appear. The man, however, for some reason or other remained in his rooms, and our hero at length muttered:

"All right, I have him treed. I can put my hand on him any time."

Oscar walked away and proceeded to Broadway, and having another matter on hand which he was quietly shadowing he went to a noted private clubhouse. He entered and lounged for some time around the parlor. His keen eyes were wandering around in restless glances—not that he was directly looking for anything, but it was a habit, and as it will be demonstrated it was a useful habit in a man of his profession. He observed two strangers enter the assembly-room and later go with a club [Pg 35] member to the café. This was not an unusual incident, and possibly might have passed off as intended by certain parties but for one fatal error. Just as the men passed through a doorway the clubman turned and took a measuring glance at our hero. The keen detective noted the fact which to him was significant, and he muttered:

"Hello! what does this mean?"

Oscar's mind acted rapidly. He reviewed all the facts. He had just entered the club; he had come from a close "shadow;" two men entered immediately after him; he had never seen either of the men in the clubhouse before; they addressed one of the members and the three passed from the general sitting-room, but not until the clubman had taken a suggestive glance at our hero, and this latter fact was very significant—it meant something. Oscar did not recognize the club member. He had seen him, however, several times in the clubhouse, and was satisfied that the man was really a member. But who were the other two men, and why had they directed attention toward him? This was the question at that moment. Oscar retired to one of the private club-rooms. He wrought a marvelous change in his appearance. It was one of the most magical transforms ever attempted, and having worked the change he descended to the café. In the club our hero was not known as a detective. He was registered there as a matter of business, and had adopted but one initial, taking his middle name, so that under no circumstances would Woodford Dunne and Oscar Dunne be recognized as the same person. The club to him was a convenience for "fly" purposes. Once in the café he saw the two men and the club member seated at a table engaged in earnest conversation, and he heard the club member say:

"I still insist that you have made a mistake."

"How?" [Pg 36]

"In the crowd you lost your man and have trailed the wrong man."

"I am certain he is the same man."

"But I know the man."

"Who is he?"

"I asked his name a few days ago. His name is Woodford Dunne. He is not an officer—a bank clerk, I think, or possibly a traveling salesman. One thing is certain: he was not trailing your man, not trailing any one."

The man who had asked "Who is he?" was thoughtful a moment and then said:

"Our danger may be greater than you imagine."

"Nonsense!"

"I say yes."

"How?"

"Are you dead certain that man Woodford Dunne is not in this club to shadow *you*?"

The man addressed turned pale—very pale.

"How long have you known him as a member?"

"I am certain he has been a member for a number of months."

"It's all very strange. I tell you we have made no mistake. That man was listening at the door of Wadleigh, and it is Mrs. Wadleigh that we expect to employ. He came from Wadleigh's rooms, where he had been peeping, to this clubhouse."

The men were talking in very low tones. Oscar had sneaked in and had not been observed by them, so intensely were they engrossed in their talk. He had dropped into a seat near them and had picked up a paper.

"How do you know he was listening at Wadleigh's keyhole?"

"You know our orders. Having agreed to employ Mrs. Wadleigh, the governor gave us orders to shadow Wadleigh. We have been on his track. I was going to take [Pg 37] a peep and a listen, and silently ascended the stairs when I saw I had been anticipated. I slipped back to the street and we lay around. That man who you say is Dunne came from the house and we followed him here."

"He may have come from some other part of the house."

"I would like to think so, but I know better. He lay around after he left the house for Wadleigh to come forth, but we managed to give Wadleigh a tip and he stayed in his rooms. There is no mistake; the man Woodford Dunne was the man we saw dodging at Wadleigh's keyhole. What his real lay was I don't know, and we might assume it was an off play but for the fact that he came here. *You* are here. Is he not on your shadow? That's what I want to know."

"This is very serious."

"Yes, it is."

"We must go into this man Dunne."

"We must."

"And if your suspicions are correct the flag of the clubhouse must soon float at half mast for a dead member. We cannot afford to be tripped up now."

"That is true."

At this moment one of the men for the first time observed the presence of our hero. They had no reason to suspect that the man reading the paper understood the subject matter of their discourse and again, they did not realize how distinctly in their engrossment they had spoken. The presence of the club member did not give them much concern, but they changed their theme.

Oscar still maintained his position, and strange thoughts were running through his mind. He had obtained the information that many supposedly reputable men were in the great steal, and here he had evidence that a member of a very respectable social club was possibly in the great [Pg 38] organization. It was not a startling discovery in one sense, for the police records will show that many a man who lived a reputable life before the great public for many years has been in the end discovered to be a cool, calculating rogue in alliance with criminals. Even while we write this statement one of these disclosures has been made to a startled public. Accident unmasked a millionaire, a man who has posed before the public for twenty years, and this accidental discovery led to the positive proof that this same man has been a systematic criminal for years; and even after having acquired a million he continued his evil criminal game until exposure came, as it is always sure to come and overtake the guilty sooner or later.

The men left the café. Oscar had a good lead and he knew he must go very slowly, as he had some very keen men to deal with. Again he went to a private room and worked back to Mr. Woodford Dunne. He had played his little game around the men and determined to let them play moth around his light.

A little later he left the clubhouse. He had determined to give the men a chance. Instead of being a shadower he learned that he was being "shadowed." He had been there before. He could stand a shadow as well as he could shadow others. He determined to give the men a fair show, a better show than he usually got when playing the same game. He went to a well-known gambling place. There was not a resort in New York City that our hero could not locate, and in every one of these resorts, under one guise or another, he had an *entrée*. In some places he was known under one character, and in others under a very different guise. He had laid out all this piping for as many different emergencies. Having become a detective, he made the methods of his profession an exact science. Oscar had not been long in the gambling den when his original suspicions were all fully [Pg 39] confirmed. The two men who had shadowed him to the club entered, and our hero mentally argued:

"Those fellows certainly stick to my identity."

The detective engaged in the game. He was not a gambler—he abhorred gambling. He had seen so many men drop down to poverty who had taken their first step back in a gambling den, and during the course of his career he had warned, and in some instances saved young clerks who were just beginning to slide downward. Gambling is a fatal amusement and sooner or later leads to disaster. Oscar, however, knew how to gamble. He had learned the various games merely as aids in his profession, for most criminals are inveterate gamblers, and it is in gambling dens where detectives find their richest fields for "dead shadows."

A few moments after Oscar had gotten into the game one of the men who were shadowing him also got in. It proved to be a very commonplace play. No large bets were made, no great sums were lost or won. The shadower had managed to crowd in beside our hero, and Oscar had favored him in securing the seat, and as was expected the man opened a conversation.

"A slow game," he said.

"Very," answered our hero laconically.

"I don't like this faro anyhow," said the man.

"It passes time."

"I prefer a good game of draw."

Oscar detected that the man was just playing a good game of *draw*—he was trying to *draw* our hero into a private little game of draw-poker; but it was not the poker that he wanted to inaugurate. His game was to draw our hero to some convenient place where he could play a still more significant game of *draw*.

"I like a game of draw myself," said Oscar, nowise loath to favor the man's game. [Pg 40]

The detective did not know where it was all leading to, or what it was leading up to as a final denouement, but he was inured to the taking of desperate chances. Peril was a pastime to him. He was ever watchful and always prepared for danger.

"I think I've seen you before," said the man.

"Where?"

"I can't recall; possibly in some club."

Our hero had detected that he was dealing with a very smart man—a man of nerve and coolness—a man who went slow but sure. He also discerned that it was to be a play of skill and experience in roguery against experience and skill in detective work.

"Let's take a little of their whisky," said the man. "It's about all we can get out of this game."

Oscar, having set out to be led, rose from the table, cashed in his checks, as his whilom friend did, and followed to the sideboard where they were joined by the second man, and number one said:

"My friend Thatford. I don't know your name, sir."

"Woodford Dunne," answered our hero promptly.

"Yes, I've heard the name. I reckon you are acquainted with some friend of mine, for I've certainly heard the name."

The men had poured out their drink, when number one, who had announced his own name as Girard, said:

"That's mighty poor whisky. It's like the game—bad."

Thatford said:

"Let's go and have a little lunch and a good drink to wash out that vile stuff."

"Will you go with us?" said Girard.

"You must excuse me, gentlemen; I am a stranger. I cannot thrust myself upon you."

"It's no thrusting; we would be glad to have you join [Pg 41] us. Thatford and I are no strangers in New York. Really, I am glad to have met you. I know a good fellow when I meet him. I am a sort of mind reader in picking out thoroughbreds."

"If you will excuse me, gentlemen, I will decline your invitation. I thought I'd drop around to the theater and see the closing act."

"That ain't a bad scheme. We'll go with you and have a little cold snack afterward."

As the men had invited our hero to accompany them he could not well refuse to permit them to accompany him, especially in view of the little plan he had settled to act in regard to them.

The three men did proceed to a theater, and our hero was surprised to see one of the men, Girard, bow to a very innocent-looking and beautiful girl who was in a private box in company with quite a stylish party. Girard was a good-looking man and he dressed with faultless taste. No one would suspect him as a rogue on his appearance, and besides his manners were excellent—quite gentlemanly.

Oscar fixed his gaze on the fair girl between whom and Girard the nod of recognition had passed, and as he stood there in the theater he revolved in his mind the singular facts. He wondered how a man of Girard's polished exterior should have been chosen to act the spy on a common confederate rogue.

Later he was destined to learn why Girard had been selected.

When the curtain went down on the last act Girard said:

"Thatford, you will have to excuse me to-night. I see a lady friend here. I may receive an invitation to dine with the party she accompanies."

"I won't excuse you," said Thatford.

"Our friend here will keep you company."

"No, you must go with me." [Pg 42]

"Where will you go?"

"To the Brunswick."

"I may join you later."

Oscar discerned the fine play that was being worked on him. He fell to the whole business, and more keenly appreciated what an excellent actor the man Girard really was.

"I fear I will have to beg off," said Oscar.

"No, no, gentleman, this will not do. I am as hungry as a bear, but do not propose to sit down to a solitary meal. Come, Mr. Dunne, you must certainly be my guest."

"All right, sir, as you insist. I did intend to go home and retire early to-night, but recognizing how your friend here has deserted you I will go with you."

"I am obliged to you, and we will have a meal that shall amply compensate you. Girard will lose it, and when we tell him of our good time to-morrow we will make him green with envy."

"I may be with you. I am not sure yet I will receive an invitation from the other party."

"That chap," thought Oscar, "is a quick thinker. He knows how to take advantage of the slightest incident when he is playing a game. All right, he is a bright player. We shall see how to scheme against him."

Girard went away, and Thatford and Oscar proceeded to the Brunswick. The former became quite confidential after the first glass of wine, and his confidences were conventional and natural.

"My friend Girard is a great chap," he said, "one of the biggest-hearted fellows in the world. He is very rich and generous."

"He appears like a very generous man," said Oscar.

"He is just what he appears to be. He has but one weakness—he is excessively fond of draw." [Pg 43]

"Yes," thought Oscar, "he is playing a big game of draw with me, and he expects to draw me into some sort of a web. Well, he may succeed; we can't tell, Mr. Spider."

Oscar did not speak out just what he thought, but said:

"I am partial to a little game myself under the proper conditions."

"What do you consider the proper conditions?"

"My companions in the game gentlemen, who, like myself, play for the sake of amusement, and not to win for the sake of the money."

"Then Girard is your man, and I think he has taken a great fancy to you, Dunne. He is a queer fellow in some things, but when he takes a fancy to a man, he clings to him, and is always ready to do a good turn."

"That is a good trait."

"Do you know, or rather would you suspect, that he was a poor orphan, and the architect of his own great fortune?"

"No, he acts to me like a man born to wealth."

"On the contrary, he is the son of Irish parents. He was born out West. His father was a ne'er-do-well. Girard at the age of twelve started in to provide for his mother and brothers and sisters. He went to Chicago and got in with a firm on the produce exchange. He served them well for several years and saved money until he could speculate on his own account. He is an honorable fellow. He resigned his position the moment he started in to deal on his own account, and he moved right along, making little successes, until finally he had money enough to go in for a big strike. He caught the market just right and at the age of twenty-eight got out of business with half a million to the right side of his hank account. He then came on to New York, and here he has lead an easy life, just enjoying himself in a quiet way; and, as I said, his great weakness is poker. He don't play a heavy game, [Pg 44] but loses with a good grace and wins with exceeding courtesy."

"I reckon he must be a pretty good fellow."

"He is, and hang me, if we are not going to have the pleasure of his company. That pretty girl did not ring him into her party, and he has come to make things pleasant for us. I am glad he is here."

Girard, looking as innocent and jovial as a "let her go easy," honest man, joined Oscar and Thatford, and started in with a pretty compliment, saying:

"Well, gentlemen, I got left, but I am stranded on a pleasant shore when my 'renig' sends me to such excellent company and such a bountiful repast."

CHAPTER V.

THE GAME GOES ON AND FINE PLAY IS DISPLAYED ON BOTH SIDES.

"Well, you are a good one," thought Oscar, and he mentally questioned whether or not he was coming out ahead of such a bold schemer, for the detective was well aware that the invitation business was a misleader—what is called a "fake." The fellow really intended to gain time to put up his job for "doing" our hero, in case it was decided that he was to be "done up." Herein Girard had the advantage. He had fixed his plan and our hero was going it blind, not having had time to arrange a trick against the one he well knew was being set up for him.

Girard sat down and commenced a lively talk. He spoke in glowing terms of the lady who had recognized him in the theater. Indeed, he was as jolly and pleasant as a man who had no evil design in his heart. [Pg 45]

The meal was finally concluded. Oscar had placed his end of it well and appeared about as jolly as a man should appear who had imbibed his share of several bottles of wine.

"What shall we do?" asked Girard. "I don't wish to go to bed; I prefer having a nice time. Can't we go somewhere and have a jolly little game of draw?"

Oscar was not loath. He desired to let the men draw him, believing that while they were playing their little trick he might work a little on his own hook.

"Hang it!" said our hero, "I am not in the habit of staying away from my home all night, but since I've started in I don't care what I do for the rest of the night."

"Where can we go?" asked Thatford.

"To some hotel. We will take a room," suggested Oscar. His suggestion was only a "flyer." He knew the men did not wish to go to a hotel. It was a part of their game to draw him to some place where they could open up the scheme they had in their minds.

"I have a friend who always keeps open house."

Thatford laughed and said:

"Yes, a pretty close friend. You want us to go to your bachelor quarters."

"Well, why not at my rooms? We can play as long as we please and turn in when we get ready."

"I have taken advantage of your hospitality so often I'd rather cry off," said Thatford.

"Oh, nonsense! come on. What do you say, Dunne?"

The intimacy under the influence of the wine had progressed so far that the men addressed each other as though they had been friends for years. Wine softens down the austerities and makes apparent friends with great readiness. It was decided to go to the bachelor rooms of Girard, and the three men passed to the street. Oscar meantime became quite gay and very plainly showed the effects of the wine, [Pg 46] but really he was fearfully on the alert, and when we write fearfully we mean it just as we write it; for he did not know at what moment one of the men might plunge a knife through his heart or send a bullet through his brain. He knew that their purpose was a dire one, and the only question was, how would they work out their plan? Keen were his glances under his seeming inebriety, and he beheld the men exchange glances, and also recognized looks of triumph, intimating, "We've done it well. He is ours."

The three men walked on and at length halted in front of a house which our hero had once had under suspicion.

"Here we are," said Girard.

"All right," responded Oscar.

"Say, my friend," suggested Thatford, "we must not play for large stakes. Remember I am not a rich man; I can't lose like some of you golden bucks."

"I never play for big stakes," said Girard.

The men entered the house and Girard said:

"My gambling box is on the top floor. There I don't annoy my neighbors."

"All right," said Oscar. Our hero was seemingly in a very complaisant mood. The men ascended to the top floor. Girard ushered his guests into a room which contained a full equipment for a game of draw. There were shaded lights, a polished table, and by touching a button he summoned a lackey to serve in attendance, and our seemingly half-boozed Oscar scanned the face of the lackey and perceived that indeed a very cunning game was being played. Cards, cigars, liquor, and all the paraphernalia were introduced, even to chips, and the game commenced. Our hero had started in to buy a big wad of chips, but he was restrained.

Indeed, the rascals were working the game for all it was worth in the way of a total blind, until the moment when they intended to open up. [Pg 47]

The game had proceeded for about half an hour when the attendant entered the room and made a whispered announcement to Girard. The latter appeared to be annoyed, but said:

"All right, show them up;" and turning to his guests he added:

"It's awful annoying, but a couple of my friends, knowing my habit, have dropped in. They will want to come in the game."

"The more the merrier," said Oscar.

Thus he spoke, but he realized all the same that the chances for his escape were lessening. Two more men would make it five against him, including the attendant, whom our hero had set down as a "stool" in disguise, and the inquiry arose in his mind:

"What can their game be? They have certainly gone carefully about it and have made great preparations to do me; but how do they intend to do it?"

The two men were introduced into the room. They came in seemingly in quite a merry mood, but a moment later one of them fixed his eyes on our hero, stared in a surprised way and finally asked:

"Girard, where did you come across that individual?"

There was a tableau at once.

"What do you mean? Of course you know the man."

"Here, my good fellow, I'd like to know what *you* mean?" demanded Girard.

"Do you call that man your guest?"

"I do."

"Do you know him well?"

Girard appeared very much confused and did not answer.

"Answer; do you know that man well?"

"No, I met him to-night."

All this time Oscar sat silent, but really appeared like a man who had been detected in something mean. [Pg 48]

"You don't know him well?"

"I do not."

"You met him to-night?"

"Yes."

"Who introduced him to you?"

"No one. We became acquainted by chance. But see here, this gentleman is my guest and I want you to explain."

"Oh, I'll explain."

"Please do."

"I denounce that man."

"You denounce him?"

"I do."

"On what ground?"

"He is a spy and a sneak. He will report you for keeping a gambling house. He is a sort of detective pimp, does all their dirty work. That is the man you are entertaining. Let him deny it if he will."

This was a bold accusation, and all the men glared at our hero, and finally Girard said:

"Dunne, what have you got to say for yourself? If this is false call that man a liar. It is your right, for he makes very grave charges against you."

"With your permission," said Oscar, "I will withdraw. That man's charges are not entitled to a reply from me."

"But see here, mister, that won't do."

"What won't do?"

"If his charges are true you have been playing me."

"I have been playing you?"

"Yes."

"How?"

"Well, you understand your purpose. I don't. But one thing is certain: you must make a full confession, or I will hold you responsible for any interpretation I may put upon his charges." [Pg 49]

Oscar apparently began to sober up, and he said:

"I do not choose to make any explanations."

"What do you know about this man?" demanded Girard, addressing the accuser.

"He is a reward seeker—a man who will ingratiate himself into the company of gentlemen. If he gets into a private game of cards he reports a gambling game and has gentlemen arrested. He is a general spy and sneak—a man who will go into court and perjure himself for a bribe, and he has made trouble for many a good fellow. He has hired witnesses, perjurers, at his beck and call. He is always up to some game. He is, in short, a lying, miserable rascal; that is what he is, and I know him."

"These are very grave charges," repeated Girard.

"Yes, and I will not remain to listen to them."

"But you will remain."

"I will?"

"Yes."

"Who says so?"

"I do. You shall not steal into my house to spy and sneak on me, and get away."

"What will you do about it?" asked Oscar coolly.

"What will I do about it?"

"That is my question."

"Do you admit the charges?"

"I am too much of a gentleman to deny them: they are so gross."

"Oh, you intend to get out of it that way, eh? Now who are you?"

As Girard spoke he rose from the table and presented a pistol directly at our hero's forehead. Oscar did not flinch, but asked:

"Do you intend to murder me?"

The detective was in the worst dilemma of his whole career. He knew the men were playing a game, that the [Pg 50] chances were all against him, and that the possibilities were that under one pretext or another they intended to kill him.

"No, I don't intend to murder you. I am no murderer, but I do not intend to let you get away with any sneaking purpose you may have had in working your way into this house. Are you a gentleman?"

"Yes, I am a gentleman."

"Then you shall have a chance. I challenge you; yes, sir, you must fight me."

"This is murder," said Oscar.

Our hero believed his last moment had arrived. He had braved fate too far in his enthusiasm. He had walked into a trap from which there was no escape. The duel which had been proposed he knew would only be a pretense in order to murder him. He knew he had walked right into a trap, but he determined to die game. Yes, even at that moment he did not wholly despair. These men did not know his mettle, and could he once get a weapon in his hands he would make a desperate fight. He was armed, but thought that possibly the men might go through the farce of a duel. This would give him a chance. He had his club and he knew he must take them by a grand dash, a magnificent surprise. He had encountered as many men on several occasions in desperate conflict, but these men had the "bulge" on him. They were prepared and on the alert. The chances were that every man was well armed and ready to "pull." He must get a vantage ground from where he could take them by surprise—throw them off their guard; but even then the chances were against him, for these were no ordinary men. They were a lot of cool, nervy criminals, well prepared, as stated—men who had their plans well arranged, their signals also. Possibly each man had his appointed work. They were men who could and would carry out their [Pg 51] orders. It was a desperate moment, and all the chances were against him.

It was at this most critical moment that an extraordinary incident occurred. Oscar saw but little chance; still, as intimated, he was determined to make a desperate fight even in face of the odds against him, and there he sat revolving the matter in his mind when suddenly there sounded a little tick-tick like the tick-tick of a telegraph machine. The men did not notice the tick-tick, it was so low and sounded like the involuntary cracking that is sometimes heard from dried furniture when a fire is first ignited in a room. To our hero, though, this very singular tick-tick came with a wonderful significance; indeed, to him it was a language. It was a telegraphic message, and he knew that he was all right. Indeed, he received full instructions as to what he might expect; he learned when and how he was to give a signal at the extreme moment when he needed help. We will not at present attempt to describe his surprise and his admiration of the faithful one who like his shadow must have followed on his track to do the succor act when succor was needed. Oscar did not change his demeanor. He acted as though he still feared the terrible ordeal which confronted him.

"You must fight me," said Girard, "and I show you great mercy in giving you a chance for your life."

"Why must I fight you?"

"You are a sneak. You have imposed upon my confidence. You have forced your way into my rooms, having in mind a treacherous purpose."

"I did not seek you. No, sir, you sought me; you invited me here. I declined to come. You forced yourself upon me. I did not force myself in here."

"I thought you were a gentleman."

"I am a gentleman."

"You must fight me all the same." [Pg 52]

"I can see," said Oscar, "you men are a gang of confidence men—robbers. You have inveigled me here to rob me. I will not be robbed. I will yell for the police."

One of the men aimed a revolver at our hero and said:

"Open your mouth to utter one cry and you are a dead man."

"You men dare to threaten me?"

"Yes, we dare to threaten. You shall not betray us."

"Aha! I see my conclusions are correct. You are thieves and fear betrayal."

"We only fear being belied by a rascal like you. We're all gentlemen; we have reputations. We do not desire to rest under a false imputation of being gamblers. Now then you have one chance. Tell us just who you are and your purpose and we may spare you; otherwise—" The man stopped.

"What will you do otherwise?"

"Kill you."

"See here; you men cannot double-bank me. I am not here to be robbed. I see through this farce. You rascals cannot scare me."

"Hear!" exclaimed one of the men. "He is insulting."

"Yes, he has insulted every one of us. He must fight."

Oscar laughed and asked:

"Do you wish me to fight the whole gang?"

"Hear him! he denominates us 'the gang'!"

"Certainly, you are a gang of thieves. I can see that I have been inveigled in here. This is a trumped-up charge against me; but I repeat, I defy you. Do your worst."

"Get the swords," called Girard.

"Who will fight him?"

"I will," said the attendant suddenly stepping forward. "Yes, gentlemen, I will fight him. It is not proper that [Pg 53] gentlemen like you should besmirch yourselves by fighting with a low-bred scoundrel like this fellow. I am his match; he belongs to my class. He and I will meet on equal terms. I will settle him, gentlemen, and afford you some rich and excellent amusement."

"Henri," said Girard, "you are not a swordsman."

"I will prove to you, my master, that I am swordsman enough to fight this wretch who has forced himself into your presence to act as a spy. Yes, sir, I will teach him a lesson."

Oscar could not discern what the real purpose of the men was. It appeared somewhat like a farce to him, and yet their trick was one that has often been played. They could in case of need make out that it was a case of assault, where one man had sought the life of another. Indeed, there had been several cases of a like character in New York. In one case the men had claimed that a duel had been forced upon another; and again a case had been known where it was made to appear that there had been a murderous assault, and of course there were plenty of witnesses, and the law is compelled to accept the testimony of unimpeached witnesses. While in both cases alluded to the police were convinced a cold-blooded murder had been committed, they were unable to prove it, however, and the assassins went free. Here were four men who could testify as they chose, and the chances were that as far as the courts were concerned they were reputable witnesses. The latter was the game our hero calculated the men meant to work on him. They had deliberately planned his murder, and the chances would have been dead against him but for the little tick-tick, and that singular tick-tick told a wondrous story; but even with this in his favor the chances were against Oscar when he conceived a plan as cunning as the one that was being played against him. [Pg 54]

CHAPTER VI.

OSCAR CONCEIVES A PLAN AND A RE-
MARKABLE DENOUEMENT FOLLOWS—
COOLNESS AND PLUCK WIN AGAINST
SCHEMES AND CUNNING.

Our hero finally decided upon a plan. He determined to convert an impending tragedy into a farce.

The detective smiled when the lackey volunteered to "do him up," and said:

"I see you wish a little amusement, you fellows. You shall have it. Get the swords. I am a gentleman and I will enjoy slaughtering this ambitious cocky-doodle-doo. He wishes to become mincemeat; I will gratify him. Yes, gentleman, get the swords and the fun shall begin."

The men stared. This was a turn in the affair they had not anticipated, but they were evidently prepared to meet the emergency.

"Who will act as this fellow's second?" asked Girard.

"You need not trouble yourselves, gentlemen."

"Oh, no, you must have a second. Although you are not entitled to any consideration this affair shall be conducted as though you were really a gentleman. Thatford, will you act as the fellow's second?"

"I must respectfully decline," said Thatford. "I am not acting as second in an affair of honor for a low-bred spy and sneak."

The lackey meantime had prepared himself for the affray, and Girard had produced two dueling swords. It looked serious indeed, but there was also an element of farce in the whole affair.

"I will excuse Mr. Thatford from acting as my second."

"Will you accept me?" demanded Girard.

"No, I will not accept you. I anticipated that you [Pg 55] fellows might be part of a gang of thieves and I prepared to meet you. No, no, gentlemen, you have not got this all your own way. I do not propose to be murdered like a caged rat, I assure you."

The men glared. There had come a complete change over our hero, and indeed Oscar had laid out his whole campaign.

"You fellows are thieves," he said, "thieves and murderers. I believe you are the parties who murdered a young man who has been missing for some months, and I further believe he was made a victim in some such way as you planned to make a victim of me; but, my dear rascals, I won't have it."

The men began to assume menacing attitudes, while exchanging glances.

It was evident they were surprised, but a greater surprise was in store for them as our hero exclaimed:

"The opening act is over. We will now bring on the tragedy."

Oscar stamped his foot, the door opened, and to the surprise of the men a boyish-looking youth stepped in the room. Indeed they did stare, and Oscar said:

"See, I anticipated your moves. Here is my second; this young man will see that I have fair play."

Girard here spoke up and demanded:

"Who are you? How dare you enter my house uninvited and unannounced?"

The youth assumed a merry demeanor and said:

"I thought there was going to be some fun here and I dropped in; that's all. I like a fight—a good square fight."

The men were evidently unmanned. There was something going on that they evidently did not understand. They were very shrewd men—great schemers. They believed they had played a good trick, but suddenly there [Pg 56] came a change in their belief. There had followed a succession of strange and remarkable developments which they did not understand. The mystery paralyzed them; the boldness of the move terrorized them. Indeed, Thatford, who was usually a pretty nervy man, edged toward the door, but Oscar called out:

"Hold on, mister, don't go. Remember this lackey here was to afford you some excellent amusement. He looks as though he were just the man to keep his word. He shall keep it, and afford you the amusement he promised. I will aid him. See, he is all ready; he is stripped for the fun. I do not need to strip. Give him a sword, give me a sword and we'll have gore; yes, we'll have gore. I will punish him, and then, gentlemen, I will be prepared to mix the gore. Yes, we shall have lots of amusement; it will be a roaring farce."

One of the men appeared to recover his nerve and said:

"Say, mister, you call us thieves, but I reckon you are a thief. You have undoubtedly arranged a good little game of your own."

"Oh, yes, I've arranged a good little game. I invited yonder fellow to my house to engage in a game of draw. I had three dummies ready to run on and make a trumped-up accusation. I attempted to force a duel on the man I had inveigled into my house. I had a disguised swordsman in the garb of a lackey to do the murder act. Oh, yes, I am a thief, and I planned well—so well that I have you gentlemen all at my mercy. Just witness how well I planned."

Again Oscar stamped his foot on the floor and three men entered the room, and they were fully equal to the part they were called upon to play. The rascals thus overmatched realized the neat manner in which they had been beaten. Terror filled their hearts, for they did not at the moment know how well they had been trailed down. [Pg 57] One fact was patent to them, and that was that they had put up, as they supposed, a great trick on a detective and had been outwitted in the most complete manner. There was no way out of the hole for them. Bad as they were, they knew they were not a match for the five individuals who faced them. The three men who had entered the room last were Jim terrors right on their looks, and their easy, offhand manner froze the blood in the veins of the conspirators. Girard attempted to face the matter by a display of nerve, but his attempt was pitiful in view of the situation as it at the moment confronted him.

The lackey meantime gave signs of terror. He was a swordsman, but realized that all his skill would go for naught, seeing that the game was exposed. Indeed, a most remarkable tableau was presented, but Girard tried to play out to save his *confrères*. He said:

"Well, well, Dunne, I expected to work a big scare on you, but I see you have been too smart. The next time I attempt a practical joke I will measure my intended victim better."

"Ah, you will?"

"Yes."

"Then this was all a joke?"

"Certainly; but you have proved yourself the best joker."

"You think so?"

"Yes, I am dead beat."

"And as you say it was all a joke."

"Certainly, you know it was."

"And what license had you to attempt to play such a broad joke on me?"

"Joking is my delight."

"Is it?"

"Always."

"Good enough; you tried your joke, I will now try mine. [Pg 58] I'll teach you to pick up a stranger in the street to make him the victim of your joke. Oh, yes, we will call it a joke, a good joke, but the joke is not played out yet. You have had your fun. I must have mine, and here goes!" Oscar whipped out a club. He leaped forward and down went Girard, and the other detectives also got in and there was a very lively time in that upper room for about three minutes. The thieves did not dare offer any resistance. They took their medicine and yet they were all brave men. They were only too glad under all the circumstances to get off with a good sound club-bing, and they got it. Then Oscar and his forces drew off, leaving the men to think over their discomfiture at their leisure. We say the officers withdrew. They did, all but Oscar. He thought to take a little advantage of his success, and dodged into a room adjoining the one where the remarkable scene we have described occurred. He knew the men were all well done up and would not in their bewilderment be prepared for the latest trick of the detective. Our hero's friends descended the stairs, making a great noise, and they kept addressing themselves to our hero, asking him questions in a loud tone, but he was not present to answer them. The questions were a part of his scheme to mislead the men, and his purpose was to overhear what passed between the men after they supposed that he and his companions had departed. He relied, as stated, on the demoralization of the scoundrels, and his position, as it proved, was well taken. The men did assume that he and his party had departed and they commenced talking, and our hero was at hand to overhear them talk. Girard was the first speaker.

"Great Scott!" he ejaculated, "who was looking for this? We are boys—greenhorns—compared to that fellow and a tale is told."

"Yes, a tale is told," said Thatford. "We thought we [Pg 59] had everything dead under cover. We were proceeding in fancied security, but these fellows have been on our track. This is not the scheme of a night. We have met a setback that will keep us poor for six months. We will not dare move until we ascertain just how far they are on to us."

"I knew something was up when we discovered that fellow shadowing Wadleigh. It was a lucky discovery, and our experience to-night, although rough, is a good play out in our favor. We know now just where we stand; that is, we know to a certain extent our danger."

"Not altogether, nor do they know all. Otherwise there would have been a close-in. They are on to us, but have no real points. Yes, Girard, this little experience is a good one for us. All operations must cease until our enemies are removed. We must go back to the old game and do a little dropping out and make the road clear again."

"That is just what we must do. We certainly have some information for our friends."

"We have; and there must be a meeting. All work must stop. Word must be sent out all along the line."

"Yes, sir, and at once. When will Redalli return?"

"He should be in New York within two days."

"We need his headwork; that is certain."

"We do, and you say he will be in the city within a few days."

"Yes, and one more fact: we must throw up the lease of this furnished house and seek new quarters. They have this place down."

"Well, this is only a fancy resort for us anyhow. Fortunately, there is no evidence in this house."

"No, no; I never would have brought that fellow here if we had had any evidence in the house, although I did not think for one moment that he would do us up the way he did." [Pg 60]

"He has our identities."

"He has."

"That is his advantage, but where does ours come in?"

"We have his identity."

"He will change."

"So will we, but I will know that fellow under any cover. He will not know us unless we have forgotten how to do it."

"It is easy for us to change."

"You bet; he fell to us in our best rôle."

"He did."

"But how did he get on to us at all?"

"I must have time to think that out, and mark my words: he is a shadower. He got his points down well. I am a shadower; I will be on his track, and the next time I will have my points down well. Whatever happens, that fellow must be put away."

"He is a terror."

"He is, but he had it all his own way this time. We were groping in the dark, but he had a good flashlight on us."

"He did."

"Boys, we have had our ups and downs before. We have been in bad holes, but we always managed to get out. We have had better men than this young fellow on our track, and we have always got the best of them in the end. Remember, we have for years baffled the best officers in the United States. We have no reason to be discouraged. This is only an incident; we know they are not down to facts, and before they get there we will get in some of our good work."

"You bet! How will we start in?"

"Our first object will be to identify every man who is in this raid against us. When we succeed then we will know just what to do." [Pg 61]

"Then we know how to employ our time until Redalli arrives in town."

"Yes."

"And we will lay everything before him. In the meantime there is no danger."

"Unless he may get on to Wadleigh. How much did he learn from that fellow?"

"I can give it to you that he learned nothing, for Wadleigh said nothing; it was a lucky escape."

"You have seen Wadleigh?"

"Yes, and he had something to tell me. I did not have time to talk with him because I had this scheme on hand with that fellow. Oh, I only wish I had known his game, and I would have laid a different course. He had it all his own way, as I said, when we thought we had it ours. It would have been a big thing, however, if our little trick of to-night had not miscarried. We would have had that chap in a hole that only a full confession would have gotten him out of, and then it is doubtful if we would have let him off alive."

Oscar had overheard enough, and he did not give the rascals the credit he would have done had they suspected his little dodge in listening to what they had to say after the shindy, and again, as they were to follow him he knew he could get on to them when the time came. It was to be a game of hide-and-seek, and he felt assured that with the brave and magical Cad Metti he could give them points on a double shadow. He stole down the stairs, gained the street, and as he walked away he was joined by Cad, and he said:

"Well, sis, you appeared at the right moment."

"Yes, Oscar, I feared they had some desperate game to pay. I knew your rashness. I fell to your track and when you entered that house I sought out some of our friends and had them at hand to drag you out of a bad scrape." [Pg 62]

"Sis, I was in a pretty bad scrape, and you appeared on deck at exactly the right moment."

"That is what I intended to do, but what was their purpose?"

"Cad, to tell the truth, I don't know."

"How did they get on to you?"

"They caught me peeping on the fellow Wadleigh. There is where they played it nice on me."

"What have you learned?"

"I have only picked up some leaders. We have a tangled skein to unravel, and we have got to do some pretty smart work. Those men are good ones; we are guarded at every point, and yet we have made a big stride toward a grand close-in some day, but our chance may come in some months from now."

"What lead have we?"

"I have the names of some of the king-pins. I have their identity; I know the name of the great master of this lodge of criminals. I will have his identity, and then our work will begin. They will shadow us; they have my identity. They are good shadowers, and as they said I worked in the light last time they may work in the light next time, but if they do, Cad, it will be when our lights are smashed."

Cad and Oscar proceeded to their several homes; both had worked hard, they needed rest, and it was late on the following day when they met. Before parting from Cad our hero had given her some specific orders, and when the two met they were prepared in case of an emergency to work some wonderful changes. They were prepared, as intimated, to do some magic trick detective work of the first order. Oscar had had a chance to think matters over and lay out his campaign, and when he parted from Cad he went to meet Wise, the great government special. He found his man at a hotel where he was masquerading in [Pg 63] the rôle of a merchant from St. Louis, and he also knew well how to play any rôle he started out to assume.

"Well, Oscar," said Wise, "I've been expecting you."

"Certainly."

"When will you start in?"

Oscar smiled and said:

"I thought you had started me in."

"I did, but not having heard from you I thought you might be laying back to finish up some old business."

"No, sir, I went right to work."

"You did?"

"I did."

"Well?"

"I've made some progress."

"You have?"

"I have."

"Let's hear about it."

"I've shadowed down to several of the men."

"Oh, you have?"

"Yes."

"Well, my dear fellow, we did that, but it's the king-pins we want."

"So you told me, and it was the king-pins I went for."

"Eh! what's that?"

"I know the name of the chief center of the whole gang. I am on his track; I've got the identity of his aids."

"You think you have."

"I know I have."

"Oscar Dunne don't talk unless he knows what he is talking about."

"I know what I am talking about this time."

"Let's hear your tale of woe."

"Not yet. I only came to tell you that within three days I hope to introduce you to the king-pin—the chief man—the director of the whole business." [Pg 64]

"If you can do that you have accomplished one of the greatest detective feats of the age."

"I will do it, sure. I've got all the lieutenants identified, got their names and their muggs. I've got them shadowing me. Within an hour they will be on my track. How is that?"

"It's great."

"Watch them on my track. You know what it means."

"I think I do; you will really be on theirs."

"Yes, and I've some big surprises for them. I've learned their plans, they are ready to spread a flood of counterfeits of every description. They have got all their plans complete. I will be on to their plans in a few days, and we can close in on them just as they let go their first dove."

"If you are correct you are at the top of the profession. I'd like particulars."

"In a few days, I'll give you all the particulars and your men."

Oscar went away. He had gotten up so as to be recognized. He sauntered on to Broadway when a lady approached. She was veiled and she asked:

"Is this Mr. Oscar Dunne?"

The detective was taken a little aback, but answered:

"May I inquire why you ask?"

"If this is Mr. Oscar Dunne, the detective, I have some business with you."

"We will suppose I am the man you seek; what is your business?"

"Will you accompany me?"

"No."

"I thought you were a detective."

"Suppose I am."

"It's your business to listen to one who seeks your aid."

"Go on, I am listening." [Pg 65]

"There are reasons why I do not wish to talk on the public street."

Oscar was only sparring for time; he was measuring the woman, and he had not gotten on to her purpose when he said:

"Where do you wish me to go?"

"To any public place where we can sit down and I can relate to you my strange and remarkable experience. You will decide that I need aid and advice. I have been told that you are just the man to aid and advise me."

"Who sent you to me?"

"A friend."

"What is your friend's name."

"A Miss Lamb."

Oscar did know a Miss Lamb. He had once done her a great service, and the woman's answer rather threw him at sea in his conclusions.

CHAPTER VII.

CAD METTI AND OSCAR PERFORM SOME GREAT TRICKS AND AT EVERY STEP GAIN IN-FORMATION LEADING TOWARD A THRILL-ING DENOUEMENT.

The detective was compelled to think quickly, and yet he sought a little time.

"Miss Lamb sent you to me?"

"Yes."

"You are a friend of Miss Lamb?"

"I am."

"Tell me about her."

"She is a deserving young woman working honorably for an honorable living." [Pg 66]

"And she sent you to me?"

"She did."

"You desire my services?"

"I do."

"Madam, I am very busy."

"You will have time to advise me."

"Is advice all you need?"

"That depends."

"Upon what?"

"Upon what you may conclude after you have listened to my narrative."

Our hero had decided on his course. He decided to go with the woman and permit her to tell her tale, for as the matter stood he could arrive at no positive conclusion concerning her.

"Where shall we go?" he asked.

"We will go to some prominent restaurant."

"But, madam, I have not seen your face."

"There is no reason why I should not remove my veil. I will do so when we are seated at a table. Let me tell you my experience is a very strange one. I have a very extraordinary story to relate. I know you will become interested; I know you will decide to serve me if you will only let me narrate my startling experience."

"You shall certainly have an opportunity to relate your experience, madam."

"Miss Lamb told me I could rely upon your generosity, but let me tell you I do not expect that you will serve me simply in a spirit of chivalry. If you can extricate me from my very singular entanglement I will be in a position to reward you in the most munificent manner, but it will require brains, courage and coolness to release me."

"Madam, I will not claim any of these qualities in advance, but I will accompany you and listen to your strange tale. I am interested in odd experiences; it is my infirmity." [Pg 67]

"I have been informed that you have no infirmities; that you are a bold, resolute, keen, level-headed gentleman."

Our hero smiled and said:

"Shall I select the place where we shall go?"

"If you please."

"You do not seek privacy?"

"Only so far as I can relate my story and be heard by you alone, and let me tell you I may do you a great service while you are serving me."

"That will be splendid," said Oscar.

He walked with the veiled woman to a well-known restaurant. He led her to a table in a remote corner, and the moment they were seated she removed her veil and disclosed a very beautiful face. She was evidently an American woman, and our hero had detected a Yankee pronunciation, but he was thoughtful enough to know that the down east idiom might be assumed. We will here say that his suspicions of the woman had not relaxed, but when he beheld her fair, beautiful face his suspicion was just a little staggered.

As indicated, Oscar had not dismissed his suspicions entirely, and he waited wonderingly for the woman to open up her business.

"You have never beheld my face before?" she said.

"Never."

"It may seem bold for a positive stranger to ask a favor, but as I said this is a matter which requires very delicate manipulation. I cannot trust every one, not even among the corps of detectives."

"And yet you feel that you can trust me?"

"Yes."

"Why?"

"I believe that combined with shrewdness, courage and cunning you possess a sympathetic nature." [Pg 68]

"You are very complimentary."

"My informant was Miss Lamb."

"Miss Lamb has evidently spoken very kindly of me."

"Yes, she thinks you are a fine type of honorable manhood."

"Miss, please do not compliment me any further through your acquaintance with Miss Lamb. Please explain the nature of the business that led you to seek me."

"Before I explain my business to you I must exact a promise."

"I am careful about making promises."

"Yes, I know as a detective you are not at liberty to make promises off-hand, but my case is a very peculiar one."

"What do you wish me to promise?"

"I have a very remarkable disclosure to make; probably one of the most remarkable disclosures you ever listened to during the whole course of your professional career. It is a disclosure that will call for very prompt measures on your part. It is a disclosure that will make you professionally one of the most famous detective officers in the world."

Oscar stared and wondered what could be the nature of this thrilling disclosure. He said nothing, but kept upon a line of intense thought, and the woman proceeding said:

"Some very prominent people will be involved—men who stand high, who will be torn from their high estate. I am willing that you should perform your full professional duty, save as concerns one individual, and I want you to promise that you will save that one individual, though he may be the most guilty of the whole gang of criminals."

The woman's proposition was suggested, and it was a most remarkable one.

"Can you promise?" she asked. [Pg 69]

"I cannot."

"Then my lips must remain sealed."

"I am sorry, miss, but I cannot promise to spare a criminal. I am bound by professional honor to close in on every criminal whom I can convict."

"Then, as I said, my lips must remain sealed."

"What are your relations to the individual who is a criminal and whom you desire exempted from the consequences of his acts?"

"He is my brother. Yes, sir, and in coming to you I am betraying my dear brother; but I would do so only to save him from the consequences of his crime. If I cannot save him I cannot betray him, but I do think that when I reveal to you the plot and identities of many criminals in return I should receive the promise of the exemption of one of them—that one, my own brother."

"I will not positively declare that I will not make the promise; it will depend upon the nature of the disclosure. Will you indicate the character of the disclosure you have to make?"

"I will."

"Do so."

"There is existing in this city a band, an organized gang of the most skillful criminals on earth. Their organization is so complete that a discipline as perfect as military order prevails. These men have defied the police for years; they are doing more harm to the commercial world than ever was suffered before in many years. My brother is a member of this gang. Misfortune overtook him, and in a moment of desperation he became a member, a sworn member. He is very useful to them, owing to his skill in certain directions. He has made a confidant of me. He has told me everything and I, after a long struggle with myself, determined to save him if I could by betraying his confederates. I know all their identities. [Pg 70] I know all their plans. I can place them bound hand and foot in your power, but my brother must be saved. It is to save him that I am prepared to make the terrible disclosure. You will become famous; you will achieve a professional victory where all other detectives have failed. You will do the country a service such as no detective ever before performed, but the price of my disclosure is the salvation of my brother."

"Why do you not cause your brother to withdraw from these criminals?"

"I cannot. I have exhausted my persuasion with him. He is mad, mad, believes he is on the eve of the acquirement of great wealth. To be rich is his mania. He is really insane. I wish to save him. I can do so only by a betrayal of his confederates, and a disclosure of all their plans and devices as revealed to me by my brother."

Oscar was amazed in spite of his inurement to surprises. He was aghast at the suggestions involved in the woman's proposition, and he had cause for deep study. It was a singular fact that from the first moment the beautiful woman spoke to him he associated her with the matter he had in hand, but did not anticipate that her connection with the subject would come in the strange, weird shape that it did.

"It is your brother you wish to save?"

"Yes."

"And he is associated with this gang of criminals?"

"Yes."

"He has revealed everything to you?"

"He has."

"And you wish to betray these men?"

"I do."

"Why?"

"In order to save my brother."

"You have no other motive?" [Pg 71]

"I have no other motive."

"But you told me there might be a large reward for me."

"I did."

"What did you mean?"

"The government has offered a large reward for the arrest and conviction of these men."

"How did you learn the fact?"

"My brother told me."

"Tell me more about yourself."

"I may, on one condition."

"What is the condition?"

"Can I hope?"

"Hope in what manner?"

"That you will agree to save my brother, and—" The woman stopped short.

"Proceed, miss, you have another proviso."

"I have."

"State it."

"Can I hope that you will save my brother under any circumstances, and share the reward with me? for without my aid you cannot earn it. I should be entitled to at least one-half of the reward."

"Miss, if through any information you give me I earn the reward I will share with you."

"And my brother?"

"I may be led to recognize that I can promise to spare your brother on the ground that criminals are sometimes promised immunity upon turning state's evidence."

"My brother is not a criminal," answered the beautiful young lady in an earnest tone.

"He is not a criminal?"

"No."

"But you have admitted that he is a member of this dangerous gang."

"He is, but he is not a criminal." [Pg 72]

"How will you demonstrate that?"

"In a moment of desperation, while actually insane, he was seduced to become a member of the gang, but he is an honorable young man. Were it not for his trouble he never would have dreamed of converting his wonderful skill to the services of these bad men."

"He is skillful."

"He is."

"In what direction?"

"Alas! I must have your answer before I tell you."

"And I must know about you and your brother before I give the answer."

"Can I hope?"

"Yes."

"You will entertain the proposition to save him and divide with me?"

"Yes, I will entertain the proposition, but I will not promise until I know more."

"Under any circumstances you will not use the information against my brother if I only partially explain to you?"

"I can make no promises."

"I must have some guarantee."

"I can give no guarantee until I know more."

"Oh, what shall I do?" exclaimed the woman.

"Trust me; trust in my honor."

A moment the beautiful lady meditated and then said:

"Yes, I will trust you. I can do nothing else."

"I do not think you will have reason to regret trusting me."

"My father lives in Massachusetts. He is an engraver. My brother inherited a marvelous talent for engraving, but he detested the employment. He went into other business, and met a very beautiful and accomplished girl. He was to be married when he lost his position. It mad [Pg 73] dened him, and in a desperate moment he fell in with one of the members of this gang. He was beguiled into betraying the fact of his wonderful skill as an engraver. He had no idea at the time of offering his services, but they induced him to show them a specimen of his handiwork. Then they offered him splendid inducements to join them, promising him a fortune. He was dazzled; he saw a way to win a fortune and his bride, and he yielded to the temptation. He has produced some wonderful plates. I do not believe his equal lives on the face of the earth at his craft."

The story told by the woman was probable and reasonable, and it did appear that our hero was about to secure men and evidence in a most strange, remarkable, and complete manner.

"Where do you reside?" asked Oscar.

"I am temporarily residing in New York. I am studying typewriting. I hope to be able to earn my own living as a typewriter, but it would be a grand thing for me if I could secure a few hundred dollars out of the reward."

"Is it your desire to obtain the reward, or is it your main purpose to save your brother?"

"It is my main purpose to save my brother. I do not care for the reward on my own account solely, but with it I can send my brother away. I believe he will learn a lesson that will last him all his life when those men are arrested and punished. And with the money he will have a chance to make a fresh start in some other city."

Oscar thought the matter over, and we will admit that there was no doubt in his mind as to the genuineness of the story he had listened to. It did not appear that there was the least possibility of its being a false tale. It was not the beautiful face of the narrator and proposer that had led him to this conclusion. It was the probability and reasonableness of the story itself; but with his usual [Pg 74] caution he determined to investigate. He was not prepared to accept any statement, no matter how probable and reasonable, without absolute proof. Still, as intimated, there was no question in his mind as to the genuineness of the information and the sincerity of the proposition.

"How do you intend to proceed?" he asked.

"In order to obtain the reward you must not only secure the men but convict them," said the beauty.

"That is true."

Oscar was a little disturbed here at the girl's singular knowledge and shrewdness.

"These men have constant meetings with my brother."

"Where?"

"At the little house where I and my brother reside."

"Where is that house located?"

"In Brooklyn."

"And these men go to your home?"

"Yes."

"Do they know you are acquainted with the purpose of their visits?"

"No."

"Are the plates in this house?"

"No."

"Where are they?"

"I do not know. I only propose to furnish you the opening clues and let you follow them up and find the plates and all the evidence."

"Your brother knows where the plates are concealed?"

"He does."

"Can you not secure the information from him?"

"I cannot. I have tried to do so, but he tells me he is bound by terrible oaths not to reveal where the workshop is located."

"He never works at your home?"

"Never. He is often gone away all night. I think they work at night." [Pg 75]

"Then how can I locate them?"

"You can trail my brother. Shadow the men also whom you will meet at our home."

"I am to go to your house?"

"Yes."

"When?"

"Any time you may elect."

"And then?"

"I will conceal you. You can see the men who come to talk with my brother. You can overhear all that passes. You can identify them and shadow them. I think they go from our house to the secret workshop."

"I will arrange with you to go to your home."

"When?"

"At some future time."

"Very soon?"

"Yes."

"Within forty-eight hours?"

"Yes."

"And I have your promise that under no circumstances is my brother to be arrested?"

"We may arrest him and let him turn state's evidence."

"No, no, never. I am only anxious to save him from disgrace. I am revealing this to you in order to save him from disgrace. Yes, it is for this purpose I am betraying his confederates."

"Can you meet me to-night?"

"I can."

"I must have time to think this matter over."

"We must act quickly."

"Yes."

"It would be better were you to make arrangements to go to my house by to-morrow night at the latest."

"Yes, I will."

"Where shall I meet you to-night?" [Pg 76]

"Here. We have dined together; we will sup together."

"We will meet near here?"

"Yes."

A corner was named and a little later the woman, who did not give her name, and our hero separated. Later Oscar called upon Miss Lamb. He learned from her that she had met a lady at the typewriting school where Miss Lamb was a substitute teacher, and Miss Lamb had really referred the lady to our hero upon gaining her confidence, and having learned that she had need of a detective in a very delicate affair, the nature of which had not been revealed to Miss Lamb.

When the detective parted from Miss Lamb he was more and more convinced that the beautiful sister of the criminal was honest, and really intended to put him on a "lay" that would indeed advance him to the top rung of the profession.

An hour later Oscar met Cad, who wore a very serious look upon her face, and she waited for a little time, when with a glitter in her eyes she demanded:

"Who was that creature you dined with to-day?"

Oscar laughed in a merry way. He read the thoughts that were chasing through Cad's mind, or, rather, he *imagined* he did so.

"Did you see her, Cad?"

"Yes."

"Did you mark her beautiful, innocent face?"

"Her innocent face?" repeated Cad in a sneering tone.

"Yes, innocent face."

Cad fixed her brilliant black eyes on her partner, and her lovely face was ashen white and her voice trembled as she asked in what might be termed a husky voice:

"Are you joking, Oscar, or were you really deceived?"

"I was not deceived, Cad."

There came a look of relief to the Italian girl's face as she said in a less sharp tone [Pg 77] :

"What a goose I was; certainly you were not deceived by that vixen."

Oscar started.

"What do you mean, Cad?"

Again there came a glitter to the girl's eyes as she said in a cold, incisive tone:

"Oscar, I really believe you are in earnest, and were deceived by that expert schemer. Brother, that woman was playing you for a fool and I see you were played."

CHAPTER VIII.

OSCAR AND CAD PLAY SOME FINE DETEC-
TIVE WORK AGAINST THE CUTEST ROGUE
THAT EVER SET OUT TO DOWN A DETECTIVE.

"Cad, what do you mean?" demanded Oscar.

"I mean just what I say, brother."

"You saw that lovely girl?"

"I did.".

"Did you hear her strange tale?"

"I did not; but I watched her face while she was talking to you."

"I did not see you."

"No, I did not come under your gaze."

"And you did see the lovely lady who was talking to me?"

"I did."

"And what was your conclusion?"

"My conclusion was and is that she is one of the most subtle deceivers that ever set out to hoodwink a good man, for she succeeded."

Again Oscar laughed and the glitter in Cad's eyes became even more brilliant as Oscar said: [Pg 78]

"Cad, had you overheard her story you would not think me quite as big a fool as it appears you do."

"Tell me the story," said Cad in sharp, quick tones.

Oscar did repeat word for word all that had passed between him and the woman and then added:

"You see, Cad, how for once you have reached a too hasty conclusion. That woman was really doing us a great service. I'll bet my life on her sincerity."

"You will?"

"I will."

"It's lucky I am here to save you from being trapped. Oscar, I am ashamed of you, but a blond beauty can fool any man, that is plain, and that woman has fooled you."

"Nonsense, Cad."

"I see through the whole scheme."

"You do?"

"I do."

"All right, sister; I will never pooh-pooh anything you say, but this time you are at fault."

"I am, eh?"

"Yes, you are."

"Are you sure?"

"I am sure."

"Oscar, I've a revelation for you."

Oscar's face assumed a serious expression, and Cad continued:

"My dear brother, I was on that woman's track when she accosted you. I am on to their whole scheme, for I have been at work."

Oscar stared and then said slowly:

"I am to meet her to-night."

"Certainly, you will meet her, but when you do will you know her game? She is the beautiful siren who is to lure Ulysses into the den where he is to be slain with merciless precision and cold-blooded exactness." [Pg 79]

Again Oscar stared, but seeing the glitter in Cad's eyes he fell to a conclusion and asked:

"Is my beautiful partner jealous?"

"Yes, I am jealous for your life. I do not wish to see you beguiled and imperiled by that woman."

"Cad, you speak like one who knows what she is talking about."

"I do."

"Have you information?"

"I have."

"Forgive me."

"No, there is no need to ask forgiveness, but let me tell you something: this little game they are playing is one of the shrewdest tricks ever attempted. I would have been deceived; you are deceived, for a more reasonable and probable tale has never been told; and yet, Oscar, that woman is the right bower of the criminals. Her fertile brain conceived the whole plan to entrap you. It is the play of these men to remove every one inimical to their success, and they, having marked your identity, have conceived a scheme to drop you out. They know you are dangerous. I know you are brave, strong, and valiant, but they have arranged a plan against which courage and cunning count as naught."

"You are sure, Cad?"

"I am sure."

"What are you on to?"

"I am jealous for your safety, and after those men had your identity I determined to get on the track of the man Girard. He is a wonderful man in his way. I followed him; I saw him dispatch a messenger boy. I kept upon his trail."

"Under what disguise were you?"

Cad laughed.

"Great ginger! Cad, can it be possible?" [Pg 80]

Again Cad laughed and said:

"Yes, I was at hand."

"You were the messenger boy?"

"I was."

"Girl, don't call Girard a wonder. You are the wonder of the age; but go on."

"I carried his message, and the sweet-faced girl who has been giving you the beautiful tale concerning her enchanted brother is the party to whom I carried the message. They met, and under a changed disguise I overheard a part of their scheme. I saw her when she accosted you, and I knew that from you I would learn enough to connect the whole plan; I have."

"And what is their plan?"

"That girl's purpose is to win your absolute confidence. She has a party who will represent her brother, and by degrees and methods of her own, aided by her confederates, they will run down our side of it, and then at the last moment every one of us will be separately lured and done up. And they will make their plans so there will be no help for us, or rather there would be no help for us did they catch us unawares. But that they will never do; we will catch them in their own netting."

"Oh, Cad, how much I owe to you! and now what shall I do?"

"Meet her, and I will wager that there will be some of her gang hovering around. We can play a very ingenious trick and open up their scheme."

"How will you do it?"

"I can make up for you."

"You can do it perfectly."

"To-night I will go to meet this siren."

"No, no, I will meet her."

"Yes, you shall meet her, but listen: I will go to meet her; you will be on *my* track. You will see who will fol [Pg 81] low me, believing that they are following you. We can arrange where, at a given point, I will disappear and you will reappear, and then when you go to meet this siren you will know just exactly how the ground lays. You will have the whole business down on them."

"Cad, this is a great scheme."

"It is, if we play it out right. This girl will be working you for an innocent; you can afford to give her a great deal of information, and—" The girl stopped short.

"Go on," said Oscar, "what will you be doing?"

"Why, man, between us, matching them at their own game, we will get the identities of every member of the gang. We will learn where their shops and where their plates are."

"How will we do it?"

"We will know just whom to shadow for each separate bit of information."

"By ginger! you are right."

"Now that you are up to this siren's movements I can trust you, Oscar."

"I might have gotten on to her plans. I was not about to surrender on demand, but it is better as it is. Time is saved, and to-night we will work our scheme. You shall be Oscar; I will be Cad, and at the proper moment we will resume and let the game go on."

"That is my idea."

That night at the proper hour an individual who looked very much like Oscar might have been seen hovering in the vicinity of the restaurant where the interview between the detective and the siren was to take place.

Our readers can grasp what was going on. Oscar, gotten up as a female, was on the "shadow," and very speedily all that Cad Metti had told him was confirmed. He saw two men following his talented counterfeit, and he followed them, and at the proper moment rejoined [Pg 82] Cad. The second change was made and Oscar proceeded to the restaurant to meet the siren. He found her at the appointed place, and together they entered the dining-room and took seats at the same table where they had held their original consultation. The woman appeared to be in excellent humor and said:

"Oh, I feel so greatly encouraged."

"I will encourage you still further. I have considered the matter and I have determined to rescue your brother, but I must have your full confidence. What is your name?"

"Libbie Van Zant."

"Very well, Miss Van Zant, when am I to meet your brother?"

"You are not to meet him right away."

"Why not?"

"I do not wish him to suspect that I have betrayed him. I must have time to prepare him for the meeting with you."

"That is all right."

"And now let me tell you something: these are very desperate men; you must secure aid."

"Oh, certainly."

"I want you to select the men who will aid you. We must not make a mistake. You must have men with you when you make the raid on the place."

"I certainly will."

"Will you introduce them to me?"

"Why should I introduce them to you?"

"I wish to know them, so I can arrange for my brother's safety."

"Oh, I see; well, in good time you shall meet them."

"We must go slow and sure in this matter."

"Oh, certainly, and you are becoming quite a detective."

"I am working for my brother's safety—his salvation. I am willing to brave almost everything to save him." [Pg 83]

"We will save him."

"By to-morrow I will arrange for my brother to have a meeting with some of those men with whom he is associated, and I will arrange that you shall be hidden in a place from where you can overhear everything that is said. You will secure considerable information. You will know how to use it. Yes, we will move slowly, but surely. There must be no mistake made, no failure, or it will cost my brother's life, and I also may become their victim."

"Very well, you can depend upon me."

"I have your confidence?"

"Yes."

"Can we not arrange signals between us?"

"Certainly."

"I am going to start in as a regular detective in this affair, and at any moment I may want to signal to you; yes, warn you in case anything appears to be going wrong at a critical moment."

"I am delighted to work with one as shrewd and thoughtful as you are," said Oscar.

"Can you not come to my home to-morrow?"

"I fear I will not have time."

"We must practice those signals. I will not ask you to visit me across the river. I have the privilege of receiving company at the rooms of a friend of mine in this city. If we could meet there some time to-morrow morning, you might bring one or two of your friends with you and we will practice the signals together."

"All right, it is not a bad idea."

"Then I will take a walk in Washington Parade ground to-morrow at about eleven o'clock, and you shall meet me and I will lead you to my friend's room, and then and there we will complete all our arrangements. Yes, yes, I will save my brother and earn the money to start him out on an honest course." [Pg 84]

"Your affection for your brother appears to be very great."

"It is. I idolize him."

"Then at eleven o'clock to-morrow we are to meet by chance."

"Yes."

Our hero and the siren separated. She said she was to meet her brother who was to accompany her to her home. The siren passed out ahead of our hero after a merry good-night. When Oscar came forth he had wrought a change. He stepped down to the curb and glanced. He saw a little chalk mark. It would have looked to an ordinary observer like a mere accidental scrape of chalk. To Oscar it spoke volumes, and he knew that his faithful strategist had succeeded in falling to a trail; and he knew that he would soon be on the trail like a sleuthhound following its prey. The detective started forward. At the first street corner he drew a little mask lantern and flashed its light around quickly and deftly, and there again under its glare he beheld a tiny chalk mark.

"Right," he muttered as he read his sign and moved on; and so he proceeded until he arrived at a certain corner, when he came to a halt; and a few moments later a messenger boy came up close to him and said in a low tone:

"She met her man."

"Well?"

"They went in that house across the street."

"Great Scott!" ejaculated Oscar, "are you sure, Cad?"

"Yes."

"The woman and how many men?"

"One man only."

"And that man?"

"Was Girard."

"Sis, you can call up our aids and have them ready." [Pg 85]

"We can snake them into the house."

"It's lucky; yes, it's lucky, Cad, and yet, it's risky."

"Why?"

"Credo may be in with them."

"But he knows you hold his life as it were in your hands, and — —"

"Well?"

"He knows if you have trailed these fellows down so close that there is no show for him and he will be on your side."

"By ginger! you are right, so here goes. We are down on these people for fair now."

"We are, Oscar."

Cad Metti, the strange, weird girl, who could flit from place to place like a shadow, who could change her appearances as readily as a change actress on the stage, glided away, and our hero, who also, as our readers will recall, had worked a change, boldly went to the house which Cad had indicated as the place where the woman and Girard had entered. He stepped into the dark hall of the house, and then quickly worked a second change; then he stepped to the street. The house was one well known to the police; its character, we will say, was established as the headquarters for the lowest sort of rogues. The owner pretended to keep a respectable hotel. He had rooms to let, and on the first floor he ran a barroom, and although the building itself was an old tumble-down affair the barroom was quite expensively fitted up.

Oscar staggered into the house, and as good luck would have it only the proprietor of the place was present at the moment and he was acting as bartender. Oscar staggered up to the bar, his eyes rolling in his head, but as they rolled, under their seemingly drunken glare shot forth a keen, observant glance.

As stated, he staggered up to the bar and fell over on to his elbows, demanding a drink. [Pg 86]

"Where's your pile?" came the answer from the proprietor, a fellow named Credo, who was a good-looking octoroon.

Oscar displayed a big roll of bills.

"All right; what will you have?"

"Whisky."

The man placed a bottle and glasses on the bar when the detective reached over, caught the man's eye, and said in a very low but sharp, decisive tone:

"Mart, on your life, look to business now."

The man started, his swarthy face assumed a ghastly hue, and there came a look of terror to his eyes.

"You know me?"

"It's Dunne."

"Yes."

"What's your pull to-night?"

"You have visitors in your house."

The man trembled.

"Are you sure?"

"Yes, and mark me, I know it all; yes, all. There is nothing for you in it only through me. Mark well my words: I can trust you; if not, it's bad for you."

"What is it you're after?"

"I am close down on this whole business."

"What business?"

"You want it straight?"

"Yes."

"*Redalli*."

Credo fell back like a man suddenly surprised. He appeared for an instant to lose his breath, but he managed to almost gasp:

"Are you on to that?"

"I am on to the whole scheme and just ready to close in. I tell you there is nothing for you in it, and you're lucky." [Pg 87]

"I am?"

"Yes."

"How?"

"You will make a good stake through me."

"What do you want?"

"I want to overhear every word that is spoken here to-night."

"You are dead on to it all?"

"I am."

"Good enough, I am with you, and you know that when I say so I mean what I say."

"I do."

"You shall have the whole business if it's opened up here to-night. Follow me."

CHAPTER IX

LUCK AND SKILL RUN OUR HERO INTO A GREAT "OPENING" ON TO THE BIG ORGANI-ZATION, AND LIGHT STRIKES IN VERY DARK CORNERS.

It is not necessary to explain to our readers our hero's great hold on the man Credo; but he knew his man well and knew that when Credo said, "I am with you," the fellow did mean just what he said. Credo led our hero to a rear room and once there he remarked:

"It's dead against me what I am doing. I had a big stake in this enterprise."

"You haven't lost one, old man, the lines are drawn close."

"That's all right so far; but is it necessary that I tumble from anything you may pick up to-night?"

"No, you are safe; you will not come into it."

The man's face was at once wreathed into a smile. [Pg 88]

"I know you, Mr. Dunne."

"Yes, and I mean it. You will not in any way be involved."

"They need never know that I keeled 'em over?"

"Never."

"You know your business. When you talk you know what you say. I am satisfied, and I am going to let you into a secret, Mr. Dunne. I can fix you out just lovely. You will have the whole business, for the king-pin is to be here to-night. You'll get the muggs of all the big men. If you were ready to close in you couldn't have a better chance; for as I said the king-pins will all be here to-night. But I don't see how I can run clear of suspicion."

"I tell you that in no way will you be involved. I will open up from another quarter. What I pick up here to-night is only side evidence. I've got almost all I need."

"And you won't forget me?"

"No, sir."

"You know I've always been faithful."

"You have, and it's a good streak of luck that they covied right here in your den."

"Yes, they have covied here for a long time."

"Are you into this affair?"

"Only partially. I am not one of them, but they have paid me well; never asked me to go in."

"Then you can't locate anything?"

"Only the men."

"You know them all?"

"Only the big fellows, and they will all be here to-night. Their big gun, the boss of all of them, is in town, and to-night he receives reports up there. Yes, sir, you will get it all. Is it luck or Dunne?"

"It's a little of both, old man."

"You've got it good, that's all. You are against the [Pg 89] deck every time, and I did not look to you for a drop in on this thing—no, never. But you've got it all; yes, sir, that's certain."

The man Credo carefully locked the door leading into the room where he and the detective stood. He then disclosed a remarkable sight to Dunne. He slid aside a movable panel covered with paper at the side of the projecting fireplace and revealed a door. Oscar stared.

"You see, I like to know what's going on, Mr. Dunne. I made this little arrangement myself. No out knows of it but you. This opens into the chimney, and there you see a spiral staircase that leads up to the room where the meetings are held. When these chaps come here I always give them that one room, and I have gathered some strange secrets at the head of those steps. You see I've let each party into the arrangements of the room where they meet. They think I have prepared for them a wonderful meeting place. I have arranged for escapes to the roof. Indeed, I've got all manner of ingenious contrivances for them; but you and I are the only ones who know of this little arrangement here. Yes, I am credited for picking up a great deal of criminal news. There's where I get it, up there, and there is where you will get it to-night. I've given you the whole business, Mr. Dunne."

Oscar fixed his keen eyes on his man, and a cold chill ran around our hero's heart. He knew in some things he could trust the man, and he also knew that his own death would relieve Credo of many terrors. He knew that away down in his heart Credo hated him, and there was something suspicious in the revelation the man was making. It struck our hero that the fellow was acting with too much readiness. There was no need for the man to discover this very important secret. Was it possible that Credo was putting up a job to do away with the man who held him in his power? It was indeed possible at least, [Pg 90] and our hero was slow and cautious. He did not intend to be trapped like a mouse nibbling at a piece of cheese. The idea of honor among thieves is a myth. A rogue is a rogue all the time, and criminals will betray a companion or a friend ninety-nine times out of a hundred. There is no romance in crime; it is always a dark record.

"Credo," said Oscar, "you have it nicely arranged here."

"Yes, sir, it's perfect for the matter you have in hand."

"What matter have you in hand?"

"You know."

"Do I?"

"Yes."

"Well?"

"I get the information and trade it. I've traded valuable information to you."

"That is true, and between us it is business. You were not aware that I was on to this arrangement?"

The man stared.

"No, I was not."

"Well, I am going to avail myself of this trick staircase, but keep very shady. Some of the lads are outside; they must not close in if I am gone some time. Give them a signal when they rush in, or they might do something rash. The rest of the fellows have not the confidence in you that I have, and they might suspect something. Be on the lookout, and if necessary show one of them where I am, for my orders have been very strict."

There was no misunderstanding on the part of Credo. He smiled and said:

"I take what you mean. No, no, I've no such notion. It's business with us; that's right. I am not going to free myself this way, and here it is on the square. I'd rather make a stake this way, for if a man dies, he dies sudden—he don't linger." [Pg 91]

"We understand then?"

"Yes."

"All right, I am going to take in the meeting upstairs."

Oscar drew his mask lantern, slipped into the opening after a thorough examination of the whole contrivance and then he said:

"Close the door, old man, close the door."

The door did close and immediately our hero opened it. He looked out and said:

"Play very close to-night, Credo: don't let your customers, if you have any, fall to us."

"The people are all at a ball. I'll have no visitors to-night except it may be a straggler."

"All right, close the door."

Oscar believed he had taken every precaution, and indeed he had; and under all the circumstances he was very cool, but for him it was a big night and the most important consequences were destined to follow, and he knew it.

With his lantern properly adjusted he ascended the stairs and in good time arrived at the place where he was to take in his news. He had been fully instructed and he found everything just as the man Credo had stated. Well, the arrangement was indeed a good one, and he mentally concluded:

"That fellow Credo is a genius; it's a pity he is not an honest man."

Oscar could see into the room and could overhear every word—almost hear a whisper, so cunningly had the eavesdropping trap been contrived. Oscar peeped in, and there was his siren, and there also was his whilom friend Girard. He and the siren were alone. Both wore a pleased look upon their faces; they were in a merry mood, and the man Girard said as our hero got fixed to take in their sayings:

"He thinks himself a very smart fellow." [Pg 92]

"Don't make any mistake; he is a smart fellow—the smartest fellow that ever started out to shadow us, and he would be too much for us but for one fact."

"And what is that?"

"He is honest and sympathetic, otherwise I would never have succeeded in fooling and getting him in tow, but now I've got him."

"You feel assured of that?"

"I do. I've secured him on the only weak side he's got. He is the hardest man to secure I ever started out to gain, but I've gone for him on just the right tack. I will handle him with care; I will learn all he knows. I will learn just who is working in with him, and then——"

"What then?"

"Alas! it's sad to think of it. He is a good fellow, but he must *walk the plank* like the rest of them."

"Look out you don't lose your heart to him."

The woman laughed in a merry manner and said:

"I've won his. I can read it in his eyes."

"Woman's vanity," thought Oscar, and he did mutter: "That is her weakest point."

"You have measured pretty well. What is your conclusion?"

"I'll tell you; he is going it alone. He is the only one who has any points on us; of that I am certain. But, as I said, I'll woo until I know just who is in with him, if any one."

At that moment the talk was interrupted and three men entered the room. Well, our hero was surprised. One of the men he recognized at a glance and he muttered: "Can it be possible?"

As the three men entered Girard rose to his feet and greeted the man whom our hero had recognized. He exclaimed as he extended his hand:

"Redalli, I am glad to greet you, and let me tell you that you have arrived just in time." [Pg 93]

"Bah! I've heard all about it. You gentlemen are too easily frightened. There is nothing to fear."

"That man is now known as Redalli, eh?" muttered Oscar, and there came a gleam in his eyes which few could read.

"We do not scare, as easily as you think, Redalli. I tell you there is a man on our track who is quietly running us down, and if we do not dispose of him he will spoil all our work of years."

"We will dispose of him; but what have you gentlemen been doing? Why did you not dispose of him?"

"We have completed our plans."

Girard proceeded and related all the arrangements for disposing of Oscar and all the other men who might be working with him. Redalli listened attentively and finally said:

"That is all right; but, gentlemen, we will make a fortune anyhow. We can move on while these men are locating us. We are all ready to shoot forth one of the greatest floods ever sent driving over this or any other land; in fact we will sweep over Canada and Mexico. I have managed our affair, I believe, in a satisfactory manner. One day this week all the agents will be in New York. We will distribute the stuff and send them abroad. The sweep will commence in three days. Under our present arrangements we will have gathered in several millions of dollars. No such plan was ever attempted or worked out."

"How many agents are there?"

"There are eleven men."

"And where are all the documents?"

"Here in New York."

"Where are the plates?"

"The plates are all here in New York."

"Where will the distribution be made?" [Pg 94]

"I have secured a furnished house. In that house we will have all the goods and all the plates. The latter we will bury in the cellar, there to lie forever until New York shall crumble and some future archæologist digs them up from the ruins to be put on the shelves of some future museum. Yes, everything is complete."

"But these detectives?"

"We will go ahead and dispose of them. There must be no mistake. We will secure them, take them on board a vessel we can secure, run them out to sea, hang them and throw their bodies heavily-weighted overboard. That is the plan; so let our good girl there, Libbie, carry out her plan. I am here now; there will be no surprises, no rushing in of detectives. I will have a well-armed and drilled force who will nail them all, and we will quietly dispose of them. The game is all in our own hands. We have nothing to fear. Our organization is too large, too far-reaching; and when once we have made the sweep we will make good our agreements and free every member of the gang that has been arrested. Yes, we will free them all, and as to the officers we will say good-by to them after the sweep and sail away to enjoy a heaven such as Mahomet has described. Yes, it's all right; let Libbie play her game. In another ten days the cyclone will have passed and we will all be rich men—rich as Monte Cristos, dead sure."

Oscar could hardly believe his own ears. It was the most wonderful "pick-up" of his whole career; and again was it proven how crime, in spite of the most skillful precautions, is always sure to walk into its own trap in the end.

Our hero lay low for over an hour and learned some additional facts of the utmost importance. Indeed, he had men and evidence. He knew it would be the greatest close-in since a detective force had been organized. It [Pg 95] would beat all records. He had the names of every one of the leaders. He had the lead-up to the places where the manufactured goods were to be stored. He had the hour when the gang would assemble, and he determined upon one of the most dramatic of denouements.

Oscar stole down the stairs. He passed to the door of the room and summoned Credo. To the man he said:

"Credo, your fortune is made, unless — — "

"I understand. You need not fear me when I know you have them dead to rights, as you must have them after a lay-in up in that eavesdropping den of mine. No, no, they will get no hint from me. I am not in with that gang. I am in with you, and you've got 'em, and I am glad. They have not used me right anyhow."

"Then you fully understand?"

"I do."

"All right."

Oscar stole forth and Cad Metti joined him.

"What have you made out, Oscar?"

"Cad, we've worked up the job of our lives. We've got the whole business. Now then, you lay to my trail, for I must shadow Redalli."

"You've got him?"

"Yes."

"And the woman?"

"You were right. She is a siren indeed, but I will amuse her. Good-night for the present. Go, for here comes our game." [Pg 96]

CHAPTER X.

OSCAR MAKES GOOD HIS PROMISE AND AIDED BY CAD METTI, THE WONDERFUL FEMALE DETECTIVE, PERFORMS ONE OF THE GREATEST FEATS IN ALL DETECTIVE RECORDS.

Like a night sprite Cad glided away and Oscar fell to the shadow of the man Redalli. He followed him to the Hoboken ferry, crossed on the same boat with him, and saw him enter a house situated in the midst of a large plot of ground covered by lines of trees.

The detective was satisfied. He had the meeting-house, as he called it, located. He had Redalli located, and he started back toward the ferry and had gone but a few squares when he was joined by Cad and another detective. Cad was in her ordinary garb as a well-dressed young miss, only that she wore a veil drawn down over her face.

"It's all right," said our hero. He was jubilant, and he proceeded to relate all that had passed while he sat listening in the Credo eyrie.

It was well on toward three o'clock in the morning when the party walked on board the boat to return to New York, and they had just seated themselves on the boat when a party of roughs, numbering seven or eight, entered the cabin. The men were very boisterous and ready for a muss, as the saying goes. They talked loud and laughed violently, and soon their eyes rested on the three detectives. The two males as they were gotten up did not look like very formidable individuals, and the fact that Cad was veiled attracted their attention. They ranged themselves on the seats directly opposite to where the three detectives were located and our hero at once detected that there was going to be a jolly row—jolly as far he [Pg 97] and his companions were concerned—for both the men were athletes and boxers, of the first order. To them the knocking down of two or three ordinary men was a mere pastime, and as our readers know the wonderful Cad was not much behind when it came to a shindy. She could have given the famous strong woman who a few years ago appeared on the stage points in many athletic feats. One of the men looking over toward Cad said:

"There's a beauty."

The detectives exchanged looks.

They had taken the measures of the rowdies.

"How do you know?" asked one of the men.

"I'll bet on it."

"You will?"'

"Yes."

"How will you prove it?"

"I'll prove."

"How?"

"That's my end of it."

"You'll bet she is a beauty?"

"Yes, I will."

"How much?"

"A bottle."

"And you are to prove it?"

"Yes."

"I'll take the bet."

The fellow who had offered to make the bet immediately rose, crossed the cabin to where Cad sat and said:

"Say, miss, you've heard the bet. Raise your veil and let me win. I know you are a beauty."

The men all laughed. They thought it evidently the joke of their lives; to them it was immense.

It was so destined to turn out. Immense was no name for what followed, and it is very unfortunate that similar roysterers do not run up against a like party. [Pg 98]

"Come, miss," urged the man, "I've paid you a compliment. You ain't a-going to let me lose my bet?"

Cad paid no attention to the fellow, and his companions jeered. One said:

"She daren't raise her veil, or she'll make you lose, sure."

The man who had bet exclaimed:

"You've lost; I've got a bottle on you."

"Not yet; come, miss, you won't see me lose."

All this time the two detectives had sat silent. They knew what would follow, and just when to come in with the sledge hammer part of the farce. Yes, they were ready in good time to play the anvil chorus on the heads of the lively gang of insulters. It was just their pie, as the slang phrase has it.

"You've lost," cried the better.

"Come, come, miss, do you hear what he says? I know you're a beaut. Raise your veil and give me the laugh on him."

Cad sat mute, and finally the man said:

"I can't lose; I've got to see your face if I lift your veil myself."

"Yes, yes, raise and expose her mugg," cried one; "if she were a beaut she would'nt let you lose that way. Lift her veil."

It was time for Oscar to interfere and he said:

"That will do, young fellow."

"Will it?" cried the man in a fierce tone.

"Yes."

"What have you got to say about it anyhow?"

"This lady is in my company, under my protection."

"Oh, is she?"

"She is."

"Well, here goes."

The man grabbed Cad's veil and raised it, disclosing [Pg 99] her really lovely face, and at the same instant he uttered a yell of triumph, but the next moment he roared forth a yell of pain and rage, for Oscar had leaped to his feet, dealt the man a clipper square on the nose and over he went. The rest of the gang immediately set up a yell, leaped to their feet and made a rush, and the next instant there followed a regular young riot, but the fun of the thing was all on one side. The other officer also leaped to his feet and started in on the tattoo act. He just swung around like a revolving wheel with distended cogs, and every time he revolved down went one of the men, and Cad just stood up on the seat and laughed. The laugh in fact had bounded over to the opposite side of the cabin from where it first started. As the men who were downed attempted to regain their feet they got it again, and got it good. The two detectives having dropped the rascals with their fists gave them the balance of their dose with leather, and they did leather them well, kicking them over the floor of the cabin like stuffed bladders. The deck hands heard the noise, ran to the doors, and taking in the situation remained aloof. They were glad to see the rowdies get a whacking; glad that for once the assailants had run up against the wrong crowd. The rowdies bled and yelled, bled for their impertinence, yelled in dismay and terror, for they feared they would be beaten to death. They pleaded for mercy, and all the time the ferry boat kept on its way; and about the time our friends had fun enough the boat slid into her slip, and with a merry good-night to the discomfited and bleeding insulters Oscar and his friends proceeded ashore.

On the day following the incidents we have recorded our hero, Wise, the special, and several other officers held a consultation. To Wise alone did our hero reveal the importance and extent of the information he had secured, and a plan was arranged. [Pg 100]

At the time named Oscar met the woman Libbie and he played her well—played for time, for his whole plan had been changed. One thing had led up to another, and the one little racket he had at first intended to work had been put aside for a new one under the latest developments.

He parted from the woman, threw her and her friends off his track and lay low for a fresh "shadow" on Redalli, and in due time he got on the track of his man.

Several days passed, and Cad and Oscar followed their lead. Our hero several times met the woman Libbie Van Zant and made her feel very good. He played the dupe to perfection; let it appear that he was dead gone on the siren; pretended to reveal everything to her, while in fact he was just getting his points from time to time and keeping her friends under close observation through her. He had constant access to the secret room in the house of Credo, listened to a great many consultations, and at length learned just the right facts for making one of the greatest hauls in the history of crime. He trailed to the delivery of the counterfeit goods at the house in Hoboken, and had every reason to believe that the plates also were all stowed away under one roof. Indeed, it appeared in plain words as though he were destined to capture not only all the manufactured stuff, but the complete outfit of the counterfeiters, the labor of years.

On the night when the great raid was to be made Dunne met Wise and his assistants. All the plans were completed and Wise said, at a proper moment:

"Dunne, you are the detective of the age."

At the proper time the detectives one by one stole over to Hoboken. They took up their station, waiting for signals. Oscar had fallen into the wiles of the siren. She had arranged with him to take him to the house—she had played as she supposed a great card. She believed she had the name of every detective engaged on the [Pg 101] "shadow" and she became bolder; told our hero she had in the interest of her brother and the detective beguiled one of the gang; informed him that she could introduce him into the house where the whole gang was to meet; that she would be able to identify every man of them. She even professed to have fallen in love with Oscar, played the alluring siren to perfection, and it was in her company that our hero proceeded to Hoboken to be introduced into the house and hidden at a point where he could see and overhear. In talking to Girard the woman had said:

"I've got him dazzled. The man believes in me as he does in his own mother. He is like wax in my hands. I can do with him as I choose."

"Are you sure he is not fooling you?"

"Am I sure? Yes, I am sure. I will have him in that house to-night. You will discover him and drag him forth. The plan will be carried out: At the proper time the riot will commence and in the mêlée down he goes."

"I hope it is as you say. I would not chance even on your positive assurance, but Redalli says it is all right, and he is the boss. He takes the responsibility."

As intimated, Oscar started for Hoboken in company with the siren and two trusty men followed his steps. Our hero was determined that there should be no miss. He had provided against every possible contingency. He arrived at the house. Oscar had been seemingly persuaded that the siren's brother was to be their guide, that she had fooled him for his own eventual good. Arrived at the house the siren signaled and a young man, supposed to be the woman's brother, opened the door. The woman asked:

"Have they arrived?"

"No one has arrived yet."

"Then I can secrete my friend." [Pg 102]

"Certainly; but, sister, remember, I am trusting you and believe it is for your and my eventual good that I consent to act in this matter."

"You can trust me."

"If not you, whom can I trust?"

"I am acting for your good."

To Oscar the woman explained after they had entered the house that she had her brother deceived on a false "steer," but she added: "You know it is to save him."

"Oh, certainly."

Oscar was led down the stairs, led to the basement and then to the cellar. A lantern was produced and a door was disclosed, showing that an excavation had been made and a room built under the yard of the house. All the arrangements were very cunningly made. When the door was opened our hero hesitated and the woman asked:

"What is the matter?"

In a tone of fearfulness Oscar said:

"I have been betrayed."

"Betrayed?" repeated the woman.

"Yes."

"By whom?"

"*You.*"

The woman laughed and said:

"But I thought you were a man of courage. Go on; I will go with you."

Oscar delayed a moment, making some remark, until he heard a signal—a very tiny signal, but it was big and loud in its suggestions to him. He stepped into the passage and a moment later a second door opened. The secret room was disclosed and at least a dozen masked men who had been seated at a long table arose. At the instant, as our hero recoiled, the cold muzzles of two revolvers were placed on either cheek and a voice said:

"Go ahead; you can't back out now." [Pg 103]

It was a supreme moment of peril. Our hero had friends at hand, but alas! ere his friends could announce themselves the deed of horror might have been perpetrated. It was indeed a critical moment, but Oscar was cool. He stepped forward and was pushed toward a seat, and the men gathered at the table. All sat down also.

There followed a moment's silence. Oscar looked around. Near him stood the siren who had allured him into the den, and her whole expression of countenance had changed. She looked like a beautiful fiend as her eyes gleamed with delight and the red glow of triumph flushed her features. She was proud. She had promised to deliver the detective into the hands of his intending assassins, and she had made good her word.

"So you have betrayed me," said Oscar.

"Yes," answered the woman, "I have betrayed you."

"The story about your brother was a lie."

"All these gentlemen are my brothers."

"And what now, woman?"

"You have just five minutes to live. You were set to destroy us; we will destroy you."

"Poor creature," said Oscar in a tone of deep commiseration.

The woman glared, for there was a terrible significance in his tones, and she shouted:

"Down him and make sure."

Alas! the arrangements fortunately were run on seconds, not minutes, or our hero would have been a dead man. As the woman shouted "Down him!" there came a second, voice, stern and commanding:

"Hold! don't let a man move or every soul of you dies."

There was a tableau at that moment such as never has been equaled on the stage under all the complexity of colored lights. It was a scene never to be forgotten by any of the witnesses, a scene awful in its intensity of dra [Pg 104] matic effect. The woman suddenly appeared to become frozen with horror. The men removed their masks in their excitement and their pale visages shone like so many corpses as all leaned forward and listened and looked.

In the doorway stood two men, armed with repeating rifles. Behind them crowded others, and at that instant every one of those wretches know that defeat and capture stared them in the face. All their labor, all their cunning and their skill had come to naught. All realized that the greatest detective feat on record had been accomplished. All knew that there was no escape, unless quickly with their own hands they freed themselves through the grave.

The detectives filed into the room, but the siren had recovered her nerve. She saw and realized that she had not played but had been played. Quickly she drew a revolver, aimed at Oscar and fired, but our hero's quick eye detected her movement. It was not the first time he had dodged a bullet. The woman fired but the one shot. The next instant the darbies were on her tender wrists, and we will add that no resistance was offered. The men, as intimated, were well up in their trade. From the first instant they knew that in plain, vulgar language, their "jig was up." Every man quietly submitted. Life was dear to them. Every man had been behind prison walls. A surrender meant a return to jail; resistance meant death. They, as stated, all accepted the situation and quietly surrendered.

Immediately the detectives set to work to gather up their spoils and learn the full value of their wondrous victory. It proved to be a complete victory indeed. All the manufactured stock was secured, the flood of counterfeits was averted, for the well-being of the business community. The plates even that had cost thousands and thousands of dollars were captured. They were [Pg 105] never buried in the cellar to be found by some future archæologist. To conclude it was the greatest capture of counterfeiters' outfit ever made, and to Cad Metti and Oscar belonged all the credit; and from the profession and the government they received it. Dudie Dunne went up to the top as a great officer, and in a future narrative we will relate where these two wonderful people once more entered the field and accomplished great results. We will also tell the romance of the life of the bright, beautiful Italian girl who from choice became a female detective strategist.

THE END.

"OLD SLEUTH'S SPECIAL" SERIES.

The following list contains *the very latest* and best books in the detective story line, all of which are written by **"Old Sleuth,"** the best detective story writer of the age. Each book contains from 200 to 300 pages, all being bound in a new, handsome, attractive up-to-date lithographed paper cover, printed in four colors. They are for sale by every newsdealer, or they will be sent by mail, postpaid, for 25 cents each, or any five books for $1.00. Address all orders to *J. S. OGILVIE PUBLISHING COMPANY, 57 Rose Street, New York.*

1. MALCOLM; or, A Ten Day's Mystery.
2. WITCH OF MANHATTAN.
3. THE Ex-PUGILIST DETECTIVE.
4. TRUE BLUE; or, The Romance of a Great Special.
5. MURRAY, The Detective.
6. OSCAR, The Detective.
7. KEFTON; or, The Wonder of the Age.
8. A LADY SHADOWER; or, A Detective's Stratagem.
9. NIGHT AND MORNING; or, A Detective's Shadow.
10. THE KING'S DETECTIVE.
11. A PUZZLING SHADOW; or, A Detective's Enigma.
12. SETH BOND. A Lost Treasure Mystery.
13. A WEIRD SEA MYSTERY. A Detective Story.
14. THE TWIN ATHLETES. A Detective Story.
15. A SINGLE CLUE. A Detective Story.
16. A ONE NIGHT MYSTERY. A Detective Story.
17. A MAN OF MYSTERY. A Detective Story.
18. A REMARKABLE FEAT; or, Great Detective Work.
19. TALES FROM A GILDED PALACE. Illustrated.
20. A FINAL TRIUMPH; or, A Lady Bachelor.
21. MAGIC DICK, THE DETECTIVE; or, A Phenomenal Trail.
22. THE VENTRILOQUIST DETECTIVE; or, Nimble Ike and Jack the Juggler.
23. THE OLD MISER'S WARD.
24. A DETECTIVE'S DAUGHTER.
25. A WEIRD COURTSHIP.
26. WINNING A PRINCESS.
27. NORVAL, The Detective.

A $2. ⁰⁰ Book for 25 Cents!

Old Secrets and New Discoveries.

Containing Information of Rare Value for all Classes, in all Conditions of Society.

It Tells all about *Electrical Psychology*, showing how you can biologize any person, and, while under the influence, he will do anything you may wish him no matter how ridiculous it may be, and he cannot help doing it.

It Tells how to *Mesmerize*. Knowing this, you can place any person in a mesmeric sleep, and then be able to do with him as you will. This secret has been sold over and over again for $10.

It Tells how to make persons at a distance think of you — Something all lovers should know.

It Tells how you can charm all those you meet and make them love you, whether they will or not.

It Tells how Spiritualists and others can make writing appear on the arm in blood characters, as performed by Foster and all noted magicians.

It Tells how to make a cheap Galvanic Battery; how to plate and gild without a battery; how to make a candle burn all night; how to make a clock for 25 cents; how to detect counterfeit money; how to banish and prevent mosquitoes from biting; how to make yellow butter in winter; Circassian curling fluid; Sympathetic or Secret Writing Ink; Cologne Water; Artificial Honey; Stammering; how to make large noses small; to cure drunkenness; to copy letters without a press; to obtain fresh-blown flowers in winter; to make good burning candles from lard.

It Tells how to make a horse appear as though he was badly foundered; to make a horse temporarily lame; how to make him stand by his food and not eat it; how to cure a horse from the crib or sucking wind; how to put a young countenance on the horse; how to cover up the heaves; how to make him appear as if he had the glanders; how to make a true-pulling horse balk; how to nerve a horse that is lame, etc., etc. These horse secrets are being continually sold at one dollar each.

It Tells how to make the Eggs of Pharo's Serpents, from which, when lighted, though but the size of a pea, there issues from it a coiling, hissing serpent, wonderful in length and similarity to a genuine serpent.

It Tells how to make gold and silver from block tin. Also how to make impressions from coins. Also how to imitate gold and silver.

It Tells of a simple and ingenious method for copying any kind of drawing or picture. Also more wonderful still, how to print pictures from the print itself.

It Tells how to perform the Davenport Brothers' "Spirit Mysteries," so that any person can astonish an audience, as they have done. Also scores of other wonderful things of which we have no room to mention.

OLD SECRETS AND NEW DISCOVERIES is worth $2.00 to any person; but it will be mailed to any address on receipt of only 25 cents. Postage stamps taken as payment for it the same as cash. Address

J. S. OGILVIE PUBLISHING COMPANY, Box 767. 57 ROSE STREET, NEW YORK.

[Transcriber's Note: The following typographical errors in the original text have been corrected.

In Chapter I, a missing period has been added to the sentence "Criminals as a rule are fond of race betting."

In Chapter II, a missing period has been added to the sentence, "The rogues had struck a lead and so had the two sharp-eyed detectives who were playing such a neat game." A missing quotation mark has been added to the sentence, "It's a good thing, sis, to locate a rogue."

In Chapter IV, in the sentence "He knows how to take advantabge of the slightest incident when he is playing a game," the word "advantabge" has been corrected.

In Chapter VI, in the sentence "He is a terrror," the word "terrror" has been corrected.

In Chapter VII, an illegible smudge at the beginning of the sentence "moment the beautiful lady meditated and then said:" has been corrected to "A". In the sentence "I will arrrange with you to go to your home," the word "arrrange" has been corrected. In the sentence "He learned from her that she had met a lady at the typewriting school where Miss Lamb was a substitute teacher, and Miss Lamb had really referrred the lady to our hero upon gaining her confidence, and having learned that she had need of a detective in a very delicate affair, the nature of which had not been revealed to Miss Lamb," the word "referrred" has been corrected. A colon has been added at the end of the sentence "There came a look of relief to the Italian girl's face as she said in a less sharp tone".

In Chapter VIII, an extraneous period has been removed from the sentence "And what was your conclusion?." In the sentence "I know you are brave, strong, and valiant, but they have arrranged a plan against which courage and cunning count as naught," the word "arrranged" has been corrected. In the sentence, "There must be no mistake made, no failure, or it it will cost my brother's life, and I also may become their victim," the extra "it" has been removed.

In Chapter IX, a missing period has been added to the sentence "The idea of honor among thieves is a myth".

In Chapter X, in the sentence "Yes, yes, raise and expose her mugg," cried one; "if she were a beaut she would't let you lose that way," the word "would't" has been corrected. In the sentence "She saw and realized that she had not played but had been played," a comma has been corrected to a period."]